Shadow Crystals

other books and stories by Jeanette O'Hagan

Heart of the Mountain: a short novella
Blood Crystal: a novella
Stone of the Sea: a novella
Caverns of the Deep
Akrad's Children
The Herbalist's Daughter: a short story
Lakwi's Lament: a short story
Ruhanna's Flight and other stories

stories in these antholgies

Tied in Pink
Let the Sea Roar
Another Time Another Place
Glimpses of Light
Like a Girl
Mixed Blessings: Genre-lly Speaking
Crossroads
Futurevision
Tales From the Underground
Mixed Blessings: As Time Goes By
The Quatum Soul
Like a Woman
Gods of Clay
Challenge Accepted
Tales of Magic and Destiny
From the Edge

Shadow Crystals

a novella

Jeanette O'Hagan

Story 4 Under the Mountain series

By the Light Books

Shadow Crystals: a novella
By Jeanette O'Hagan
Story 4 in the Under the Mountain series

Cover design: Jeanette O'Hagan ©2019
Typesetting and Layout: Jeanette O'Hagan
Copyright Jeanette O'Hagan © 2019 http://jeanetteohagan.com

NLA Cataloguing-in-Publication entry at National Library of Australia:

A catalogue record for this book is available from the National Library of Australia

ISBN-13: 978-0-6485859-0-9

Published through By the Light Books
By the Light Books PO Box 2520, Brookside Centre, Qld 4053
Email: Bythelightbooks@gmail.com

Note: This book follows Australian style conventions for spelling, punctuation and grammar.

Subscribe to Jeanette O'Hagan's Newsletter for the latest on new releases, giveaways and other news– http://eepurl.com/bbLJKT

Dedicated to my brother, Frank,
who lives life boldly.

Delvina rubbed sea spray and sand grit from her eyes. The driving rain of the storm slackened to a sullen drizzle, and the clouds in the east showed a blush of gold-pink above the steep, dark-grey cliffs towering beside them. She couldn't stop shivering. Her clothes clung to her wet skin and water foamed over her boots.

The only gleam of hope in the whole sodden, bleak mess was the White Rose, one mast shattered, still floating in the middle of the bay. Two albatrosses, shapeshifters from the Great Forest, circled around the ship. Hopefully, the others were safe too.

'Tide's coming in.'

Delvina started at Zadeki's shout, barely audible above the thunderous roar of the waves.

Salt rimmed his eyelashes and dusted his silvery white skin. Water swirled around his ankles. He hitched his soaked sarum and knotted it tighter about his waist.

'Can you speak Eldar? What is this "tide"?' she grumped. Then took a shuddering breath.

He'd just saved her life, and she his. It wasn't Zadeki's fault that he didn't return her feelings, was in fact oblivious to them. Perhaps he had a girl among his own people. No, she needed to focus on the mission.

'I am speaking Eldar.' Zadeki flashed an apologetic smile. 'The tide is like the sea breathing in and out, following the song of the two moons, but I guess living under the mountain you wouldn't know that.'

She drew herself higher. 'You live in the forests, not by the sea.' The memory of Mariner Habbiah waiting for the tide to turn niggled at her memory, but she hadn't paid much attention when they'd left Redhaven. There had been no time to think, just the urgency to find answers for her people. Her twin, Retza, and all the others would starve if she and Danel didn't discover how to open the Gate to the Underground Realm.

'I've listened to my kin's songs of the ocean and the Lonely Isles since before I could talk.' Zadeki pointed to the white-crested wave collapsing into a slurry of foam and racing up the grey-black sand to tug at her knees. 'We need to move, the tide ... waves ... are coming in fast.'

The water fled backwards, and she wobbled as the pull scooped the sand beneath her boots.

Zadeki offered out his muscular arm. 'Let's go.'

No more than a sister. The words of rejection stabbed sharp and hard and sudden, and she pulled away.

His head tilted, and his dark brows crinkled. 'What's wrong?'

'Everything.' She let a sad laugh. 'And nothing.'

'Have I done something to offend?'

'No,' she gave a weak smile, 'No, it's nothing. Do you think Danel and the others are safe?'

'Should be. Come on, Del. We need to get to higher ground, or we'll be swimming again.'

Drowning more like. She couldn't swim.

She took his hand and they hastened across the narrow strip of sand. The sharp rocks walls, not as high as the Cauldron or as sheer, surrounded the storm-tossed bay in a tight embrace, except at the white-foamed gap to the ocean. The Grinder. She shuddered as she remembered the White Rose's perilous passage through that rock-toothed maw, the memory of being swept off the deck by a monster wave. If it hadn't been for Zadeki …

'Don't worry, Del. By the Maker's favour, things will work out. At least we are on the Big Island. Silantis won't be far. We'll soon get the answers we need.'

She stalked beside him, lips pressed together, and doubts kept to herself. Wave after wave crashed down in foaming fury and rushed at them with relentless force. Zadeki moved closer to the cliff until his shoulders were but a ninas from scraping against the slick rock covered with strange snails or some kind of shelled creature.

'Do we need to climb that?' she asked.

'Maybe not. I think they're sending a boat.'

She looked out over the churning waves. Ebed sailors were lowering a smaller boat down the side of the White Rose. Five or six people sat hunched inside as the fragile shell tilted and swayed on its journey to the churning waves below. Once it settled in the water, the boat with its high prow pushed off from the ship and made slow progress towards the shrinking shore.

One of the albatrosses peeled off and flew toward where she and Zadeki struggled along the beach.

More waves rushed up, narrowing the strip of wet sand. One rogue wave, higher than the others, slammed into them. Cold water clawed at her chest, stealing her breath. Her heart stuttered into a rapid rhythm. The water tugged and pulled and she stumbled. Maybe climbing wasn't such a bad idea.

Strong arms caught hold of her.

'Swap places,' Zadeki said. He swung her to the

cliffside as though she were a half-empty bucket. And she did feel empty, hollow. More fool her for allowing her feelings to run away with her.

'You could fly.'

'I'm not leaving you, earthbiter. Besides, I'm not sure I have enough energy to shift.'

A great silver bird with an enormous wingspan swooped down and hovered on the wind in front of them. 'Tide's coming in,' he keened.

'We noticed, Baba,' Zadeki replied. 'Where is the boat making for?'

The albatross used his sharp beak to point to a break in the smooth arc of the cliffs. A half-moon of sand shone in the fading light. 'There's a path to the top. I'll keep you company, in case you need help.'

'Thanks, Highwun Korak,' Delvina said, her breath coming in strained bursts. Water swirled around her knees.

By the time they stepped on the wider strip of sand, the water had reached Zadeki's calves and her thighs, and each retreating wave threatened to tug her under.

Delvina stopped. The sand disappeared for maybe a tanis where a gully cut into the cliffs. Fast flowing water swirled between them and the thin crescent of remaining beach.

'Jump across' Korak instructed.

A wave lifted and barrelled into Zadeki, and foaming and hissing, drenched her from head to toe. Only Zadeki's grip stopped her from tumbling over and being pulled out to sea.

Delvina gasped for air and hugged in what little warmth lingered. She couldn't move her legs. The gap was too long.

'I can't.'

Her teethed chattered and long shudders ran through

her body. The last rays of the sun glinted off the water through a rent in the clouds, but their spot remained in the deep shadow of the cliff.

'Yes, you can,' Zadeki said. 'You climbed the Cauldron, crossed the heights of the White Mountains. You called Putarn's bluff. You can do it Delvina.'

His words warmed her. She had to put her disappointment behind her. She was here for a purpose and her people were depending on her. She couldn't fail now. Pulling up the dregs of her strength and courage, she stepped back and leapt towards the sand on the other side. Zadeki pushed, giving her lift. She landed on hands and knees, water foaming and boiling around her.

Zadeki landed beside her and the albatross swooped to the sand, wings shortening and legs lengthening. Both Korak and Zadeki grabbed her arms and pulled her onto the small shelf of sand.

'Even this will be under soon,' Korak yelled.

Moments later, the boat slid up onto the sand with a hiss. Mariner Habbiah jumped out, followed by his daughter, Ariel, and Thirdwun Danel. Others followed, one of them tying the boat to a pylon.

Danel rushed toward them. 'Runner Delvina, I feared the Ocean had taken you.' His dishevelled brown hair stuck out at all angles and his clothes were stained with seawater. He squared his shoulders. 'Thank you, Zadeki for rescuing her.'

The second albatross swooped down and transformed into the angular form of Highwun Bikan. 'Brave but foolhardy.'

The Mariner grimaced. 'Never seen the like. Dived off the ship's prow like a spear seeking its target. Thought we'd lost the both of you.'

Zadeki flushed and stared at his feet.

Highwun Korak shook his son's shoulder. 'Reckless.' But the pride was unmistakable in his voice and the shine of his eyes.

'And where does he get that trait from, brother's son?' Highwun Bikan sniffed. 'But we'll get more than a soaking if we stand here much longer. We best find some shelter for the night. Storm's closing in again.'

'Aye, the path is this way,' Mariner Habbiah said. 'The White Dove is anchored and my Second, Jonan, will see to the unloading in the morning.'

Soon they were clambering up a steep, rocky path, slick with spray. Delvina shivered as the Mariner led them into the gloaming.

Danel emerged from the cottage and blinked at the grey morning light. By the time they'd reached the settlement the previous evening, it had been dark and pelting rain. The wind and rain raged outside all night, shoving against the shuttered windows, whining through the thatched roof, sneaking between the cracks. Even more disturbing, the ground still rolled under Danel's feet as though he stood on the deck of the ship of the White Rose, not on solid ground.

Now, charcoal clouds scudded across the sky and sheets of water silvered the muddied ground. A scattering of stone cottages sheltered on the leeward side of a small hill, inadequate protection against all that the open sky could throw at them. Who could have known such unpredictable and powerful forces could come out of thin air? Not a simple miner like him. He'd rather face a cave-in or groundquake in the tunnels at home, terrifying as they were. Yet more terrifying still was knowing the fate of his people depended on his ability to explain their dire situation and persuade strangers to help them. He'd had mixed results with the Tamrin and the Warden at Redhaven. He had to do better here. Failure and its consequences would be unbearable.

The sun broke through a gap in the clouds to dazzle off the turquoise water of the bay. The ship bobbed up and down like a youngwun's discarded plaything, its rear mast shattered. Circling the intact mast, white birds squawked and cried and squabbled. Too many and too small to be the Forest Folk.

'How are you this morning, son of the deep?'

Danel's heart shot up to the back of his throat and he twisted round. Highwun Korak stood in front of the weathered door, as though he'd materialised out of nothing.

Korak dipped his head. 'My apologies. I didn't not mean to scare you. Mariner Habbiah is anxious to leave for Silantis at once. I've brought you something to break your night's fast before we go.' He held out an oval-shaped object wrapped in a white cloth.

Danel's mouth watered at the warm smells. He took the food and nibbled a cautious bite. A bit like the Tamrin maizebread or the potato cakes from home, but lighter, fluffier and altogether divine. He tore off another piece with his teeth. 'This is not Silantis then?'

'A fishing village, I'd say. Silantis is to the north.' Highwun Korak pointed with his chin to the windswept hills covered with boulders and soaked yellow grass. In the distance, thick wooded slopes blended into the ragged grey sky.

More travelling. Great. The memory of the harbour

with broken and burning ships came unbidden and Danel's stomach squirmed. The Lonely Isles were under attack by unknown forces, and he only hoped this conflict didn't complicate their mission.

He swallowed down the last mouthful of food. 'What about the destruction at White Haven?'

'Habbiah's people say the fighting is confined to the eastern side of the island. We will need to be cautious.'

'Will you fly us to the capital then?'

'No, it's not that far. Habbiah is organising some land transport.'

Danel let out a relieved breath. He'd rather stick to solid ground beneath his boots, not clinging for life hanging in mid-air on Korak's koraktil.

The cottage door swung open and Delvina stepped out carrying two packs.

'There you are, Speaker Danel. Here's your pack,' Delvina said. She looked striking in her borrowed Tamrin tunic and breeches with a voluminous shawl wrapped around her. Nose peeled from sunburn and ash-blonde hair fluttering in the wind, her pale grey eyes looked determined, despite the hint of a melancholy at the corners of her generous mouth.

'Thank you, Runner Delvina.' He hastened to take the pack from her, his heart speeding up as their fingers touched.

The rest of the party trailed out of the cottage with their gear. Highwun Bikan, Zadeki, Mariner Habbiah, his daughter Ariel and two sturdy ebed servants all dressed for travel.

'So, ready to go, I hope,' Habbiah said.

An unfamiliar clip-clop sound came from the path that ran between the houses behind him, followed by a high-pitched *weeheehaha*. A pungent but sweet animal smell tickled his nose.

Delvina's pupils widened as she stared past his shoulder. 'What are those?'

Danel spun around. A middle-aged man, with the clay-coloured skin of the ebed, led two large animals linked to something like a glimmer truck made from wood shaded by a cloth canopy. Another two of the beasts were tied to the back.

'The horses, Mariner Habbiah,' the ebed said, answering Delvina's question.

Not as big as a koraktil, but bigger than the Forest Folk jaguar shapes or the Tamrin's yarmas, the horse-beasts tossed muscular necks fringed with hair, swished long tassel-like tails, and stamped the ground with rounded feet. The closest one snorted and displayed its tombstone teeth.

Danel took a step back and gulped air. 'Couldn't we walk?'

'Well, you could.' The Mariner's grey eyebrows tilted upward. 'Silantis is a good twenty lek away. Take you all day to walk, or you could be there in a couple of hours with cover of sorts from the sun, wind and the rain.'

'The horses are a bit spooked with the weather, but they'll calm down soon enough,' Ariel added.

'Will we all fit?' Delvina asked.

'Ariel and I will be riding.' The Mariner pointed at the two horse-beasts of finer build at the back. 'The rest of you can ride in the cart.' He looked askance at the Forest Folk. 'You three, no shapeshifting mind, and better cover up.'

Highwun Bikan drew herself up. 'No need to trouble yourself, rider of the waves, we will travel with the Darane.'

'Good.' He took a bundle from under his arm and tossed it at Bikan. 'Might make things smoother if you wear these.'

She caught them and shook out three long, flowing and hooded cloaks.

'What, are you trying to hide us? Zadeki scowled. He glanced at Korak, scuffed the wet grass with his sandal. 'We are not ashamed of who we are.'

Danel felt torn. The Forest Folk were their greatest advocates, but they needed the Vaane on side if they were to get the answers they needed. Why did people so obviously related, with the same tall stance and silvery-white skin, seem at such odds with each other. There was a history here that he didn't understand.

'Why are they necessary?' Delvina's eyes sparked. She rammed one hand on her hip.

'See, here,' the Mariner started. 'If I had my way, I'd leave you on the ship. No Flame-get has set foot on the Lonely Isles in ...'

'Please, son of the waves, be at peace. Despite the hot words from our youngling here, we have no objection to your request.' Highwun Bikan handed the dark cloaks to Zadeki and Korak, before donning one herself. 'Shall we go.'

The Mariner harrumphed. 'Very well, but understand you are not welcome here. Don't draw attention to yourselves. Let's get going.'

He untied the black horse from the cart and swung onto its back, speaking into its long, mobile ears. The beast gave a soft whistling sound and turned in a circle.

Danel looked askance at the cart perched high on flimsy looking wheels and shrugged. Not as solid as a glimmer truck, but probably the least of the dangers they'd face on the island. He threw his pack into the cart

and scrambled up after it. Delvina and the others
followed. Last of all, the ebed driver scrambled up and
took up the leather straps connected to the horses

'Let's go,' The Mariner rode off down the road to the
north. Ariel fell in behind him.

The driver clicked his tongue. The horses set off and
the cart jerked forward, throwing Danel against the side.

Delvina frowned. 'Why are they always so rude?'

Highwun Bikan sighed. 'Mariner Habbiah may lack
manners but, but if you wish to speak to the Sea Dragon
King, we do well to follow his directions.'

'To Silantis then,' Danel said.

Hopefully this time they'd get some the answers for
their people back home—desperately needed answers for
the littlewuns, the toolwuns and the oldwuns trapped in
the underground caverns and each day creeping closer to
starvation.

Zara sat back on the stool and stared at the rough
rock walls for the thousandth time. Her younger brother,
Jesson, slept curled up in the corner of the room, only the
messy ends of his white-blond hair peeking out from the
blanket. How many days since the groundquake, if that
was what it was? How many days since they were hustled
through the panicking throng in the Grand Cavern and
into this room somewhere below the watcher quarters
while chaos reigned above them? Ten? eleven? How
many more would be wasted here, abandoned except for
infrequent meals and the removal of wastes.

Hard to believe she missed the big drafty cavern of
the Heart Room with the constant hum of pipes and
vibration of the crystals. Though she could still feel the

Crystal Heart's thrumming at this distance, in tune with her heartbeat. They needed her because of her connection with the Crystal Heart. Without it the glimmer lights would fail, and the realm would be plunged into stifling darkness once again.

Not that her connection to the Heart did her and Jesson much good. This new prison was no bigger than a storeroom. Snug and boring. There were only so many times once could write in a journal, especially with nothing happening to write about. Either way, she was weary of being caged like a captured bird being fattened for the pot.

The gong for first shift sounded in the corridors outside. Jesson snorted and sat up. 'Do you think Retza will come with the food this time, Zuzu?' he said through a wide yawn.

Zara's pulse jumped at the mention of the former prentice turned watcher. She pushed down fluttering feelings and instead latched on to her growing irritation at her brother's incipient hero-worship.

'Jesson, remember he's the enemy. They all are.'

Besides, they hadn't seen any sign of the sturdy watcher since the first groundquake, the big one.

'But, Zara, he helped us.'

'They're rebels. They rose against our Baba, the rightful Overseer, and they're making a mess of running the realm too.'

The rebels were all hooligans, out to destroy what they couldn't understand. Uneducated savages driven by greed and envy, too lazy to better themselves. And that traitor Gilarth was up to something for sure.

Yet it had been Retza who'd saved her from Javot's lecherous intentions. Retza and the others that rescued her and Jesson from Putarn. And she had to admit, her father was not the just leader she had thought him. She gripped the table edge, pushing away the traitorous thoughts.

'Yes, but—'

The muted thud of boots came from outside the metal door.

'Hush, someone's coming.'

Moments later, Gilarth's tall figure stepped inside and closed the door behind him. He was an imposing figure in the watcher's uniform of black bat-leather, though he'd lost bulk and his face was grey with fatigue, lines more deeply etched. He leaned against the wall for a moment.

'Lady Zara. Jesson. Good to see you look well.'

Zara stood and smoothed down her skirt. 'Come to harass me again?'

A morose look flashed across the Head Watcher's face and his hand fell from the top of the truncheon attached to his belt. 'I would if I thought it would do much good. We need to know where your father is hiding or anything you know about the seal for the Gate.'

She lifted her chin and met his bronze-hard eyes without flinching, sure she was right to resist him, to remain loyal to her baba.

'Don't you hurt my sister.' Jesson rushed over and grabbed her hand.

'Nay lad, I won't. I'm doing my best to protect you both, but the more desperate things become, the harder that is.' He gave a wan smile and held out the packages of food. No doubt more stinking algae cakes. 'I've added a bit extra for the lad.' Gilarth grimaced. 'There's little enough to go around.'

She could almost believe he cared. Almost. But then why had he joined the rebels after being her personal guard for so long?

Bat-leather creaked as he moved to the door.

'Are the rumours true?' she whispered, before she could stop herself.

Gilarth threw her a quick look. He frowned.

'Well, are they?' she demanded, her voice louder.

'What rumours, Lady?' His smile was grim. 'There are as many as the glow-worms in the Grand Cavern, and I wouldn't believe most of them.'

Zara swallowed. 'That the food is running out.'

'Watcher Manoah said they'll be eating youngwuns like me next,' Jesson piped up, his face not knowing whether to be thrilled or horrified. She had hoped her brother hadn't heard that titbit.

Gilarth's brushy eyebrows mashed together. 'I'll have to have a few words with Manoah.' He smoothed his face into a smile and moderated his tone. 'Listen, no one is eating youngwuns. It was because of his plan to sacrifice youngwuns to the Dark Ones that Overseer Havilah challenged your father.' He fingered the truncheon tucked into his belt, then gave a sharp nod, as though making up his mind. 'We're short, it's true. The potato farms took blight when the Crystal Heart was out, but Lead Hand Gregan has replanted the crops and the Tamrin Abovegrounders have agreed to send us supplies.'

That didn't explain the nail-biting tension in the air, or the worry in the stance and voices and eyes of the watchers. 'Then what's the problem? And why did the ground shake a couple of days ago? Nobody tells us anything.'

Gilarth's eyes narrowed and mixed emotions flittered across his craggy face. 'Another cave-in at the tunnel.' He stepped close. 'With the Gate sealed shut, getting the supplies into the mountain is a big problem. And hauling the load up the mountains to the Cauldron won't do much good. With cliffs, and glaciers and snowstorms to contend with, it's likely they'll arrive too late to do much good.'

So, that explained the urgency. They really had made a mess of things. 'Can't you open the Gate without Baba's seal or get past them somehow?'

'We've tried both options. The Gate is booby-trapped. So Secondwun Nebam started a tunnel. The first groundquake, that was from the tunnel collapsing. Now there's been a second cave-in, more toolwuns lost.'

'If you hadn't chased Baba off, you wouldn't be in this predicament. How can you trust outsiders?' Both Baba and Da-baba insisted all abovegrounders were thieves and murderers. That going outside would anger the Dark Ones. Maybe that was the cause of the tunnel collapse. But what if Baba was wrong? No, he couldn't be.

'We don't have much choice.'

'My Baba—'

'Isn't here, Lady Zara. It's been seven rosters since he fled, six since he last sent his followers to attack.'

What if Baba wasn't coming back. What if he was … Zara stood up and paced the length of the room, fighting against her treacherous thoughts. Baba would come back.

Gilarth sucked in a long breath. 'We need to open the Gate. After the first cave-in, Overseer Havilah sent a delegation to Redhaven to seek answers from the Vaane. I only hope they return in time.'

'So Retza went with the delegation?' That would explain his absence.

A strange look flashed across Gilarth's face. 'No, Lady. He was reassigned to the rescue operations. Greenstone South, the crew on duty, were his old shift.'

'Will he come back to guard us now?' Jesson's high-pitched voice pierced the air.

Gilarth stared at the craggy roof. He clenched and unclenched his big hands.

It was a simple question, wasn't it? Her throat tightened, and the room seemed suddenly stuffy.

Gilarth's eye's shone in the low glimmerlight. He blinked. 'Retza and Secondwun Nebam were at the diggings with the second cave-in. Neither made it out.'

Didn't make it out.

The words hung in the room between them. Retza trapped, possibly dead. She shouldn't care, he was a rebel after all. But he couldn't be gone. She dropped onto the stool and clutched the edge of the table.

'You are going to rescue him. You must!' Jesson grabbed Gilarth's big hand and shook it.

'I hope so. A team is assessing whether it is feasible. With the tunnel gone, the delegation to Vaane at Redhaven may be our only hope of survival. Unless you can tell us where to find the seal.'

Zara shook her head, not sure if she could speak without her voice cracking. Why should she care that one of her gaolers wasn't coming back?

'Zara,' Gilarth's big form loomed over her. 'If you know anything, remember anything—'

'No, I don't. I don't know. I don't remember. Please, leave us alone.'

Delvina rubbed her shoulder. The cart was faster than walking, but the jolting over the rough track was as bad as the lurching of the ship tossed hither and thither by the storm. So far, only a few people had passed them on the road and there was no sign of fighting or other threats so evident on the opposite side of the island.

A strong wind blew against her face, whipping her plait behind her. Danel had taken a seat next to the driver, while she perched on the bulging sacks in the cart with the Forest Folk in the back. Highwuns Korak and Bikan sat wrapped in their cloaks on one side. Zadeki cross-legged and shredding grass on the other, his half-lidded gaze straying often to the Mariner's daughter, Ariel. Tall and slim, she rode beside her father. Her long honey-brown hair, tied loosely by a ribbon, curled in the wind. The girl glanced over her slender shoulder and smiled.

Delvina felt a hot spike of irritation. Those two would look good together. Is that why he wasn't interested in her? She clenched her hand until her fingernails dug in. Silly, it didn't matter. It was the mission that was important, saving Retza and her people.

'I'm glad we don't have to ride,' she said. 'Though the cart isn't very comfortable.

Zadeki brought his gaze back to her. 'Horses have such graceful strength. A noble form to learn.'

'Don't be in a rush to learn too many forms all at once, youngest son. You can lose yourself that way.' Korak lay half-reclined against the board, his borrowed hood casting deep shadows on his silvery-white face.

'As you say, Baba. Don't worry, I've learnt from my mistakes.'

Highwun Bikan snorted. 'One can only hope,' she said so low, it was hard to hear above the rumble of the cart.

Highwun Korak yawned. 'Conserve your strength. We might need it in Silantis.' He settled back down and closed his eyes.

The cart jolted over something big. Delvina swallowed down the rising nausea and the fizz of frustration. She focused on the sparse terrain.

The rain may have stopped, but the wind was relentless, flattening the yellow grasses coating the hillsides. Woolly animals, a bit like yarmas but with shorter necks and legs, huddled in the shelter of trees and boulders. On the left, a large conical mountain gradually came into view. Dense, ball-like trees covered its sides below a summit of grey-black rock. Soon after, two smaller peaks raised their bald heads in the distance on either side of the mud-packed road. There was no snow on their round summits and Delvina almost missed the angular mountain peaks that towered over the top of their underground realm. Here, instead of the smell of snow and mountain pines, salt and seaweed mingled with dry grass and pungent, herbaceous scents.

The white road turned to the east and she drifted in and out of sleep.

'How much further do you think?' she asked after a while.

Highwun Korak glanced at the sun, a muted silvered disc behind the ragged clouds a third of the way up the sky. 'Not much longer. Silantis should be just beyond that ridge.'

Zadeki lifted his dark eyebrows. 'I thought you'd never been here before, Baba.'

Korak waved an arm. 'Nor have I. But we have maps of the island, though they might be dated after all this time.'

'Why do you keep them, if this is no longer your home?' Delvina asked.

'It was our home once, in my mother's mother's time,' Highwun Bikan replied.

Danel twisted around on his seat at the front. 'I see a white spire ahead. Like the tower at Redhaven.'

Highwun Bikan sat up straighter, her hood slipping back from her dark hair. 'Then we approach the city.'

Soon they would know if this long journey had been worth the dangers and heartache. Delvina's pulse jogged faster.

The horses strained against a slight rise in the road.

'Will you speak for us, Highwun Bikan?' Danel asked.

'It might be best,' Bikan said. 'We know their ways and protocols. But we are here as your guides and protectors.'

'And if the Vaane allow us,' Korak muttered.

'The Maker will protect us,' Highwun Bikan said. 'I dreamt last night that the mission will be successful, though the cost might be high.'

Mariner Habbiah's horse danced beneath him, throwing her head and shaking her mane. 'Peace, Seaspray.' He stroked the beast's muscular neck. He twisted around. 'You, Flame-born, pull up your hoods and stay silent until we are granted an audience to the Sea Dragon King's spokesman, the Grand Technician. I should get you through the city without incident.'

Irritation bubbled inside Delvina. Though he spoke down to the Adelphi, he did not address Danel or herself at all.

The cart crested the ridge, and Delvina gasped at the sight of the city spread out before them.

'Silantis,' breathed Zadeki beside her.

Like Redhaven in many ways, it was a much larger and more imposing statement against the shallow bowl-like valley. Sculptured buildings with fluted columns, gilded friezes and painted murals were interspersed with open spaces, gardens, and long avenues. Together, they formed a concentric pattern, and at the centre, a large building with spires and domes sat like a jewel in a gold and ivory socket. To one side, the needle-like spire stabbed into the ragged windswept sky.

In the far distance, dark smoke billowed in the blue-grey sky. Was that White Haven burning? So close. Delvina dragged her gaze away. If both the Kapok and the Warden treated them with disdain, how would it be any different here?

The cart tilted as the road dipped down the hill and into the city.

As they approached a stone archway, two tall men in black watcher garb stepped forward. The Mariner Habbiah brought his horse to a stop, signalling the ebed driver to do the same.

'Who seeks entry to the blessed city of Silantis?' the guard with a long nose said.

'Master Mariner Habbiah and his daughter, Ariel. I bring a report to the Sea Dragon King from Warden Ealam in Redhaven.'

'Have you not heard that the Sea Dragon King is dead. Long may his heir live.'

Mariner Habbiah gasped. 'How did this happen? King Oban was not yet six hundred solars.'

'You should report to the Grand Technician. He will

no doubt tell you all you need to know.'

The older watcher spoke for the first time. 'But first, tell us how you got through the blockade.'

'We came through the Grinder. My old ship is at Destruction Bay. My Second supervises the repairs to the ship and the unloading of goods and supplies.'

One of the watchers walked toward the cart, and Delvina flinched as he leered at her. 'Are these gifts for the Throne?' He prodded a crate in the back of the cart. 'Anything dangerous.'

'Nothing the palace guards can't handle,' Ariel declared.

'As you say but go carefully. Rogue ebed have taken advantage of the confusion surrounding our great king's death. Their leaders agitate rebellion and have garnered a great following.'

Master Mariner shifted on his horse. 'This is indeed concerning news. So, these rebel ebed are blockading the harbour?'

'Yes, preventing the White Ships from sailing until the Grand Technician accepts their outrageous demands.' He gave a furtive glance at Delvina and Danel. 'You'd do well to keep an eye on your retainers.'

'Who has been appointed regent for the young heir? Not Princess Avardin?'

'The Grand Technician,' the older watcher said.

'For now.' The second watcher growled.

The other one shrugged. 'It was the late Dragon King's wish that his grandson's reign be entrusted to his old friend and spokesman.'

Habbiah bowed gracefully on his horse. 'Yes, quite wise. Thank you for your warning. May the Maker go with you.' He clicked his tongue and directed his horse down the street. The cart followed.

Once they turned the corner, Habbiah moved closer to the cart. 'We should hurry. Audiences end at noon. Unless matters have been completely upended.'

'So now we know why the White Ships stopped coming,' Bikan said.

'Aye, but not why the news of the King's death or this rebellion did not reach us through the speaking stones.' Habbiah tilted his head up at the white tower, a frown creasing his brow. 'This is a right mess, and now I wish I'd left the lot of you at the bay. Too late to worry now.'

Delvina shifted in her seat. Would this regent be more open to help them than the Sea Dragon King? Was it another obstacle or an opportunity?

'We better get a move on.' Mariner Habbiah leant forward and slapped the haunches of the nearest horse pulling the cart.

The horses leapt forward in a spurt of speed, the cart clattering along the stone-paved road.

Delvina clung on to the sides of the cart. Two ten-days since they'd left the Glittering Realms, fifteen days since the groundquake and the Overseer had sent them to speak to the Vaane. How desperate were things beneath the mountain? Was Retza safe? She shook her head and grimaced. No doubt he was enjoying parading down the causeway in watcher-black in the pursuit of his duties.

Retza clung to the digger jammed against the tunnel wall. Weariness weighed down his eyelids, his shoulders, and his spirits and shudders ripped through him. Flashing patterns drifted across the obsidian-black as his eyes strained for the smallest hint of light.

In the inky darkness, the smallest sounds echoed loud and close. The wet slap of water lapping against the digger and the wall, Peta's soft breathing, Secondwun Nebam's choked snoring, the pounding of his own heart in his ears, the rustling movements of the survivors on the island across the water. Retza swallowed hard. How long had he been down here? Only a short time compared to the survivors from the Greenstone South crew, yet already strain of clinging to the digger was taking a severe price.

He jerked out of a doze, his grip slipping and a foot splashing in the water.

'We can't remain like this.' He pulled himself up.

'Nebam's slipping away. His injuries need proper attention.' Peta's voice came from beside him.

The Secondwun's battered arm and head hadn't seemed so bad at first. Just as well they'd tied him to the digger. Even with Peta's help, he couldn't keep holding Nebam. They could barely keep themselves from slipping into the dark water.

'We have to do something,' Retza growled, to hide the tremor in his voice.

'But what?' Peta asked.

She clicked on the glimmer torch and flashed it up the tunnel. Blue-white light speared Retza's eyes and reflected off the murky water and scattered debris. Rocks, mining equipment, and temporary struts jutted out like dismembered skeletons. What if the sudden flood had smashed more supports and caused a further cave-in up the access tunnel?

'Is help coming?' Secondwun Karel's voice echoed across the lake that separated them. Desperation underscored the weakness of her tone. And no wonder, after fifteen long days trapped in this water-filled cavern.

'Not yet,' Peta yelled back. 'How are you doing?'

'We're holding on.'

But for how much longer?

Retza shivered. Eighteen survivors from the original cave-in. No chance of reaching them without some special equipment. Karel said the water surrounding their small island was way over their heads. They'd been lucky the glimmer trucks washed up against a rocky bar in the middle of the underground lake.

How many were injured? All must be weak from lack of food. So hard to measure time in the darkness without normal cues, but it had been at least two shifts, maybe even a day, since the rescue operations had failed. And what if no one was coming?

Overseer Havilah would not give up on them, especially since her son, Nebam, was trapped with them. Unless she thought they were beyond reach or dead.

Peta gripped his arm. 'I'm so sorry,' she whispered.

'Why?'

'This is my fault. As the crew's stone-singer, I should have detected the resonance of water behind the rubble. It's just ... I've never done anything like this before. The patterns were so confusing.'

She was right. It was her job to make sure operations were safe. Retza squashed the stir of anger igniting in his gut. Peta had worked three shifts straight and was working in conditions not experienced since the groundquakes some twenty years ago. Anger was not what he needed right now. 'We are going to be alright, Peta.'

He took the torch from her and flashed it down the tunnel again. 'The water level's gone down a bit.'

Peta leaned over and dipped a lift-bar into the dark water. It disappeared beneath the ripples. 'Still chest height.'

If only he could swim like the Forest Folk. If Zadeki was with them, he could fly down the tunnel to get help. Though, it was only chest height. Maybe he could walk, now the water wasn't pouring in. He had to do something. Somehow, he had to let Havilah and the others know they were still alive.

'I'm going to get help.'

Peta caught his arm. 'It's too dangerous. You don't know what's underneath the surface, or whether it gets deeper further on.'

'The tunnel rises after a while, it should be fine.'

'Then let me do it.' Peta's voice sounded gritty and determined. 'To make amends.'

'No, I'm taller and sturdier than you. And someone needs to stay with Nebam, to make sure he's alright and encourage Karel and the other Greenstone South survivors. I'm sorry, Peta. I know it's harder to stay and wait, but they need you.'

Peta's fingers released their grip. She sighed. 'Be safe, Watcher Retza. Get help. And at least take the torch.'

'Hold on until I get back.' He gripped her shoulder.

One last look around, he slipped into the ice-cold water before he could change his mind. This was the sort of crazy thing Del would suggest doing. A smile edged his lips.

He could do this. No way he was going to fail.

While the open countryside seemed deserted to Danel, the city was crowded with people. Tall people like the Forest Folk and the people of Redhaven with silvery-white skins, long flowing hair, beardless chins, and graceful robes. And shorter people, closer in statue and appearance to Delvina and himself, in brown tunics, with skin ranging from the lightest to darkest browns. Silent people, stern gaze fixed to the ground or cast over their shoulders. People hurrying about their tasks or loitering in the laneways.

The numbers of both people and buildings grew thicker as their party approached the centre of the city and it became harder for Samwin, the cart driver, to find a clear path through the press on the street. As the wind dropped, smoke and the smell of fear mixed with the subtle floral scents.

'Seems like everyone and their da-matu is in Silantis with the calamity,' Samwin muttered under his breath.

Danel nodded and turned his attention instead to the many buildings in their variety, grace and intricacy. No need for such artificial stone shells like these in the tunnels under the mountain, where spaces were hewn out of living rock. Yet he itched to replicate them in some way once he returned home. Or was it if? He sobered. If his people survived.

'Almost there, sir,' Samwin said.

The cart pulled past another building of white stone. Stairs swept up to a platform and a façade of fluted columns reaching for the sky. As they passed by, grey birds flew up from the eaves with a whirring flutter and settled back down again. A hooded person slipped back into the shadows.

Beside it, a huge ornate building reared up five stories tall. Danel recognised it as the circular central building they'd seen before entering the city. Its façade was covered in colourful murals—fierce warriors, large scaly creatures with crests on their necks and their mouths stuffed with sharp, peg-like teeth, and flying koraktil.

'Whoa.' Samwin pulled back on the reins and the cart came to a gentle stop.

'We're here.' Even brave Delvina looked subdued whether from the size and extravagance of the buildings around them or worry about the success of the mission.

Mariner Habbiah wheeled his mount around and approached the cart.

'Leave your belongings in the cart. Samwin will make sure they get to where we're staying.' He raised an eyebrow. 'Are you ready, Danel, Speaker for Darian's people?'

Was it the first time the Vaane Gentle had addressed him? All eyes turned to Danel. As Speaker, he carried the weight of the mission.

He gripped his pack and his courage with two hands and jumped down from the driver's bench. 'Let's do this, then.'

The others climbed out and stood on the street. Samwin shook the reins and headed south.

Mariner Habbiah dismounted and handed the reins of his horse to his daughter. 'Ariel, go with Samwin and open up the house. Stay indoors until I return.'

'Yes, Baba.' The girl glanced at Zadeki before urging her horse into a trot.

'The rest of you, stick close to me and don't stray.' Mariner Habbiah reached out and adjusted the hood of Zadeki's cloak, pulling it further over his head. 'The situation is fraught. Stay hidden until I say it's safe.'

Chill bumps crawled over Danel's skin. It felt like he was leaping from one crumbling ledge to another. Again, they were asking favours from strangers who seemed to have little regard for them. And this was the end of the glimmer tracks.

'We can do this, Thirdwun,' Delvina whispered behind him.

'By the Maker's favour, we'll succeed,' Zadeki added.

'Not by standing in the street,' Highwun Bikan said.

Halfway up the stairs already, Habbiah stopped and beckoned. 'Come! Hurry!'

Danel swallowed hard, brushed the pouch of gems fastened to his belt, and followed. At the grand entrance in front of them, black-clad watchers with bladed weapons briefly stopped the Master Mariner, then waved the party through.

The entrance hall was as big as the Grand Cavern, with semi-precious stones, lapis lazuli, marble and malachite. Far above them, golden sunlight shone down from a round skylight, sending faceted patterns of light and shadow skittering across the tiled floor.

'This is amazing,' Delvina whispered. 'The greenstone looks like that from northeast eleven shaft. Does all this come from the island?'

'No, daughter of the mountain, this building and hall was built from the sweat of your foremothers and forefathers, then brought across the ocean in the White Ships. Since Uzza's father rebelled against the King and shut the Gate, they've looked to the Tamrin to provide, but they are not miners and—'

'Hush.' Mariner Habbiah signalled with his hands. 'Stay here and do not move from this spot.' He pointed to a circle design in the floor. He removed his hat and approached a silverskin in brocaded flowing robes and cap. The two spoke in low voices.

'Can you fly through the skylight,' Zadeki whispered.

'Not without breaking the glass first,' Highwun Bikan replied. 'Now shush, child of the wind, before we raise the good Mariner's ire.'

'They seem an irritable bunch,' Korak said under his breath. Bikan fired him a warning look and Danel cringed. He wouldn't want Highwun Bikan angry at him.

The vast hall seemed to suck away all vibrancy and sound, leaving behind hollow traces of faint whispers, of slippers on stone, the rustle of robes, and muted conversations. Both silverskins and ebed walked past, eyes diverted from Danel and his companions, with only the occasional sideways glance. Everyone seemed on edge.

The longer they waited, the tenser Danel felt. Cave spiders spun tangled webs in his stomach. He fiddled with his belt and half-distracted himself with examining the design of cornices, archways and weight-bearing pillars. It was truly a cunning design.

'Follow me.' A man with the green cap beckoned them.

Mariner Habbiah signalled them to comply. He fell in step with Danel as they headed through more doors and passageways. The watchers scrutinised them but did not delay them.

At the end of a long corridor, gilded doors thrice the height of the Adelphi and set with crystals and precious stones, swung open. The green cap stepped in and called out 'Master Mariner Habbiah from Redhaven with his party, your Honour.'

Danel stepped into the room and shielded his eyes. At the centre of the room, a dazzling eight-sided crystal star was set into the floor. The strange design pulsed light like the Crystal Heart, only this device was many times bigger. Beyond the glare, silver and golden chairs were set on a high dais and a group of robed Vaane milled about it like seagulls circling the White Rose's two masts.

Another official stepped forward, a woman with white hair carrying a mace. 'You may approach the Grand Technician.'

The green cap waved them on, and Danel followed the woman and the Mariner around the pulsing crystals to a figure in resplendent robes standing on the stairs leading up to the dais.

Danel's eyes grew rounder the closer he got. He gasped as though his breath was knocked out from him. Surely, the Darane, the Adelphi and the Tamrin were like annoying mosquitos in the face of such power and grandeur.

Delvina gripped his hand. 'We have to persuade them.'

Danel nodded numbly, wishing that it was Nebam or Havilah standing here, that the fate of his realm wasn't in his trembling hands.

The man in robes was a little shorter than Zadeki and Highwun Korak, but he still towered over Danel and Delvina. He had a thin face with heavy lidded eyes and his white hair tied up in a knot at the back. Rainbow light threaded his robes and dazzled the eye with every little movement.

'Grand Technician Iulien and Regent of the Sea Dragon's Empire,' the white-haired woman intoned.

Mariner Habbiah knelt on one knee. 'Your Honour, I grieve the loss of our great King, may he be at rest with our foremothers and forefathers.'

'Your sentiments are admirable, Habbiah. You have a request?'

'I bear messages from Warden Ealam in Redhaven.'

'I speak for Prince Selwin and will ensure your reports are dealt with by the Star Council.'

'As you wish, your Honour.' Mariner Habbiah rose to his feet and cast a nervous look around the crowd behind him.

'How is it you sailed through the barricade, Mariner?' A regal woman with a refined face and strange opalescent eyes spoke out. 'The rebel ebed have sunk all the ships that have attempted to enter or leave Safety Bay.'

'We navigated through the rocks of the Grinder, Princess Avardin.'

A gasp ran through the group gathered in front of the dais.

'Impressive. I did not think that possible for all but the smallest craft,' the woman replied.

Mariner Habbiah inclined his head and turned back to the Grand Technician. 'Your Honour, when the White Ships stopped coming and communication through the towers and speaking stones stopped, we at Redhaven became worried. Warden Ealam of Redhaven sent me to find out what is happening. We brought some supplies, though a few were lost due to the storm.'

'You are to be commended for your bravery, Mariner. This is the first good news we've heard in over three Alume. Once you've unloaded the ship, you should sail back to Redhaven with news of our situation.'

'The ship's mast needs repairing, and the Sea Heart is depleted. But once the ship is seaworthy, I will do as you command. There is another matter I must bring before you.' He waved a silver-white hand at Danel, Delvina and the Forest Folk. 'A delegation from the Sea Dragon King's Glittering Realms.'

The Grand Technician raked Danel and his companions from head to toe. 'What, how can that be? The mines were lost over two hundred years ago. Do not toy with us.'

Danel took his cue. 'Your Honour, Overseer Havilah has sent us from the Glittering Realms to request your—'

'You are dismissed, Mariner.' The Grand Technician turned his back and beckoned to Princess Avardin to join him. Voices hummed as the others turned back to previous conversations and concerns.

'Sir, we must speak with you,' Danel raised his voice.

Highwun Bikan unlaced her grey cloak and allowed it to fold to the floor. A sense of power seemed to radiate from her. 'Son of Gaian, you will listen.' Her soft voice echoed through the eight-sided room, turning heads.

The Grand Technician spun around. 'Who are you?' His jaw slackened. 'How dare you!'

'I am Bikan, eldest daughter of the Kinleader Telsima and Pathfinder Yrsak, Elder of the Forest Folk, advocate for Overseer Havilah—'

A swell of sound fruited into a furious roar.

'Adelphi.'

'Flame-get.'

'Shapeshifters.'

'Demons.'

'What are they doing on our sacred island?'

Danel's arm-hairs lifted and his heart rammed into his mouth. Had they pushed it too far? If the Vaane attacked them now, they would not survive.

Retza sloshed through the chest-high water. He held out his truncheon in front of him, probing ahead for the debris, mining tools, shattered support struts, and overturned equipment swept along by the initial force of the water and now left in unpredictable positions in the tunnel. The rails for the glimmer tracks beneath his boots provided the best guide for the way forward in the deep darkness.

He clicked on the glimmer torch, bright light reflecting off the surface of the water and creating angular, sharp-edged shadows that confused his eye. It was often hard to distinguish an obstacle from its shadow.

One step in front of the other. He plodded along with only his memories and thoughts for company. He'd been furious with Delvina for leaving on the mission to Tarka after she'd agreed to join the watchers with him. It felt like a betrayal. They were twins, after all, and always faced life and its challenges together. Whatever happened, whether the death of their parents in a cave-in, and then Da-Baba's death, or striving to survive hand-to-mouth in the commons, they were together. Until now. He was supposed to protect her, to stick by. And he had, until she decided to leave without him. He wanted to stay mad with her, but he couldn't. If he was honest, and why not be in this extremity, he missed her.

Maybe he could have done things differently. He'd refused to go with her, given her no other option but to join the watchers. That was what he'd wanted to do, but as he probed the memory like an aching tooth, he had to admit that it wasn't what she wanted to do. Now he wished he'd listened to her concerns and been less forceful in his demands.

Not that it would have made much difference. He would still be here in this light-forsaken tunnel and she somewhere in the wide world outside. Zadeki better be keeping her safe or he would have something to say about it. If he got out of this alive.

His limbs dragged against the weight of the water. One step after the other. The sloshing of water, the constant drip drip drip of water, the wet cold grip of water seeping into every crevice and pore, into his core, wore him down. He had long stopped shivering and he could no longer feel his fingers or toes. Still the tracks went on into the receding darkness. His limbs shook and his head swam and his mind drifted.

Delvina's face, grey eyes wide with concern floated in front of him. 'Are you alright, Retza?' she murmured. Her voice faded as though moving away from him.

'What would a lowwun like you know?' Zara's lapis-blue eyes started at him, oozing accusation and disdain. 'If you'd listened to my baba you wouldn't be in this mess.'

He blinked and rubbed his eyes. He was hearing things whether from exhaustion or lack of food or the very darkness that seeped into his soul, he wasn't sure.

This was the domain of the Dark Ones, yet the Dark Ones weren't helping.

He swayed on his feet, blinking his eyes against the interweaving light and shadows.

'They require a sacrifice, trywun,' Putarn's mad voice cackled.

'No!' His shout ricocheted off wet rock and hollow spaces. He snapped his eyes open crystal shook his head to chase away the delusion.

Exhaustion pulled at him, weighing him down like stones. He stumbled and grabbed a support strut. He needed to rest, but if he did, he wouldn't be able to start again. He had to go on. Peta, Karel and the others were depending on him.

He let go and pushed out. One step in front of the other.

His boot plunged into a hole and he fell forward, arms windmilling. The water swallowed him whole. He thrashed and grabbed at everything and anything. At last a hand connected with a protruding strut. He pulled himself up, coughed up water and gulped down air.

He'd lost the glimmer torch in his panic.

How far had he come? How much further to go? All he really wanted to do was lie down and sleep. He closed his eyes. He couldn't do this on his own. He could just let go.

Somewhere water dripped on rock. And closer, the soft gurgle of running water.

'By the Maker's favour, you can do it,' Zadeki's voice whispered.

'Hold on, Retza. Hold on.' Delvina's calming voice again.

Keep going. A warm feeling bloomed in his midriff and spread, strengthening him. *Keep going.*

He squinted against the inky shadows. Dark-grey shapes broke up the black.

'I'm imagining it,' he whispered and blinked, once, twice, three times.

The patterns remained. The faintest hint of bluish light which had to be coming from somewhere.

Gathering every single tattered shred of strength, he pushed forward toward the lighter shadows. Rocks rolled beneath his feet and piled up in front of him, extending to both sides of the tunnel. A dead end.

Near the wall, a hard edge protruded, the rim of a glimmer truck by the feel. Somewhere, water trickled as if through a small gap in the rubble. Had the rush of water found a weakness in the wall, bringing down the roof on the glimmer trucks. How far did it extend?

The teasing sound of water trickling between rocks was louder here, as was the filtered blue glimmerlight high above his head.

The tunnel was blocked, but beneath an angled beam, a small gap bled glimmerlight. Which meant there might be someone on the other side.

'Help, help!' but his yell came out as a croak. He pulled himself up further until the rocks shifted under his feet. He whacked his truncheon on the rim of the glimmer truck.

Bang, bang, bang.

'Help,' his voice a little stronger.

Bang, bang, bang.

No response. Was nobody on the other side to hear his calls or to rescue him?

His hold faltered. No, he couldn't give up now.

Bang, bang, bang.

He hit the truck with all the strength he had left.

Echoes pinged around the tunnel and faded away, leaving only the loud staccato of his heartbeat and his laboured breathing.

Boom, boom, boom. Soft and distant, but an answering call.

Bang, bang, bang. His hands vibrated as he hit the truck.

Boom, boom, boom, boom.

His heart fluttered at the return message. Not an echo, but someone responding to him. Help was coming.

Retza pulled himself up as high out of the water as he could and waited for rescue.

'Flame-get, you are forbidden to step on the island,' the Grand Technician thundered.

'Violation.'

'Traitors.'

Zadeki felt the force of fear and anger swirling in the huge audience room like a mountain blizzard tearing at his wings.

If the Vaane attacked, there'd be too many to defeat, even with claws unsheathed and sharp teeth wielded. He could fly from this place, as could Baba and Aunt Bikan, but they couldn't leave the mountain dwellers behind. They were his friends and he'd sworn to protect them.

His limbs trembled with the effort not to act, to wait for Aunt Bikan or Baba's lead. He was Kin, a singer of the Forest's song and he would not let these builders of stone intimidate him.

Watchers with truncheons and whips and swords came from the archways, running towards them. Some in the crowd pulled out concealed weapons and edged towards Zadeki and his friends. He moved closer to Delvina and Danel, ready to defend them. Baba moved in closer too, his strong, steady presence like the buttress of a tall Forest giant.

'Should we fight or run?' Danel whispered, eyes white and face ashen.

'Wait,' Aunt Bikan spoke so low, her voice was more air than sound, but her meaning rang clear enough in Zadeki's mind. 'All is not lost yet.'

Baba placed two restraining hands on Danel's and Delvina's shoulders.

The cries and shouts died down and the watchers formed a ring around them.

Aunt Bikan raised her arms, her tari falling in

graceful folds to her shoulders. 'Is this how you deal with guests in your Great Hall? We come in peace, Iulien, son of Gaian.'

The Grand Technician pointed his staff at them. 'The Sea Dragon King banished all Flame-born pretenders from the Isles. You have no rights here.'

Aunt Bikan's lips thinned. 'Do you have such short memories? According to the treaty of Nakri made with your King Drako centuries ago, we have the right to be heard by the Crystal Star Council if pressing issues arise between us. This is such an occasion.'

'You come cloaked and hidden, no doubt seeking to take advantage of our great king's death,' said a burly man with a shock of hair leading a group of watchers.

'Indeed,' the Grand Technician said in a triumphant tone. 'Lord Hale has right of it. If your intentions are honourable, why hide behind cloaks?'

Warmth spread across Zadeki's neck. 'The cloaks are not our idea.' He threw his off, glad to shed the constricting and suffocating garment.

'So they are not,' Aunt Bikan agreed. 'If you would grant us a hearing.'

Mariner Habbiah coughed into his hand. 'Your Honour, Warden Ealam consented to the request to speak with you. Without the flameborn's help, the White Rose would not have reached the island or landed safely.'

A low murmur ran through the people assembled before the empty throne. The faces remained stony, their eyes accusing. These people had never met him and he had done them no wrong, yet they seemed to loathe him and his Kin as though they were monsters.

Princess Avardin stepped forward. Her multicoloured eyes skewered Zadeki for a moment before lingering longer on Baba and Aunt Bikan. She half-bowed toward Aunt Bikan with an ironic flourish. 'Forgive us, you catch us at an awkward time, Flame-daughter.' Turning, she addressed the Grand Technician. 'Iulien, should we not at least listen to this request?'

The Grand's Technician's face mottled, and he seemed about to swell up like an angry bullfrog.

The woman cut in. 'It would be in the heir's interest to know the state of his possessions over the seas. These Flameborn liaised with the Filane of the so-called Five Lands to provide us with foods and essentials.'

The Grand Technician puffed out his cheeks. 'Well—'

Lord Hale shouted over him. 'Only after stealing the Sea Dragon King's rightful dominions. The land beyond the ocean belongs to us and our Monarch. These lowborns have nothing we need. You would only show weakness to negotiate with them.'

Zadeki balled his hands into fists. The land and the ocean and the forest and the wilds belonged to the Maker and they were its stewards.

'I had not thought the children of the starshine had sunk so low as to break their sworn treaty,' Aunt Bikan's soft voice was scathing.

'Well ...' The Grand Technician smoothed down his glimmering robes. 'Ah, all good points no doubt, Princess Avardin, Lord Hale.' He inclined his head to the two that had spoken. 'And if the Warden sent them ...' He turned to Aunt Bikan, his mouth twisted as though he'd eaten something sour. 'Well, explain yourselves. What is your reason for defiling our island?'

Defile! Heat rose like lava inside Zadeki. Had not his forefathers and mothers come across the ocean with the other Vaane and lived here. His rab-da-baba Rahim had led them across the ocean. It was their island too before Doryn and his Kin were exiled.

'Are the Vaane more ignorant than the mountain dwellers and with less excuse?' he whispered.

'With less excuse,' Baba returned. 'But we must focus on the mission.'

Aunt Bikan gave him a reproving glance. She motioned Danel and Delvina forward.

'We come on behalf of Darian's people. Overseer Havilah has sent Speaker Danel and Messenger Delvina with both a proposal and a request. Once that is heard and the answer given is fulfilled, we would be pleased to leave this place, by the good Mariner's ship if possible. We have no interest how you conduct your affairs among yourself.'

'Darian's people, Gentle Bikan. You mean the rebel ebed of the mines. I thought them dead,' Princess Avardin said.

'A goodly number still work the mines and reap its riches, Sea Dragon's daughter.'

A strained silence fell over the room. Curious and disdainful eyes examined the Darane.

The Grand Technician sniffed. 'Very well, speak this message.'

'Your Honour,' Danel swallowed and took a deep breath, glancing at Delvina and then Zadeki. The young shapeshifter smiled back to encourage him. 'Your Honour, we seek your wisdom on a matter of grave importance to us and we are prepared to offer something of value in return.'

'My Lords and Ladies, Gentles,' Mariner Habbiah held up his hand. 'If you would, Warden Ealam instructed me to show you this.' He pulled out the pouch

Danel had given the Warden and emptied the contents into his cupped palm. Faceted glimmer crystals caught the light from the dome above and the Star Crystal below and sent blue sparkles shivering across suddenly avid faces. 'He assures the King—or the Crown Prince in his place—he would not have sent the ebed and children of Flame otherwise.'

The onlookers crowded closer, necks craning and eyes bright.

'Glimmer crystals,' Lady Avardin breathed. 'May I see?'

She held out a slender hand. After a moment's hesitation, Mariner Habbiah handed her one of the crystals.

'One or two minor crystals is no great find.' Lord Hale folded his arms tight against his chest and glared at Danel. 'The glimmer crystal seams were mined out just before that madman Hezikah rebelled some two hundred years ago.'

The Grand Technician clutched the lapels of his robe and nodded, 'True. These are minuscule specimens.'

'Our stone-singers found another seam some time ago, your Honour. If it's crystal you want, we can supply it. As well as many other metals and gems.'

The Grand Technician rubbed his hands together. 'Then you will cede the mines back to the Sea Dragon Throne?'

Danel tugged at his beard. 'No, your Honour.'

'No! what do you mean, 'No', ebed?' Lord Hale bellowed.

Danel stepped back, banging up against Zadeki. The Darane Speaker hooked unsteady hands into his belt and lifted his chin. 'With respect, sir. The mines now belong to us and that is something we will not give up. However, under similar terms to the Filane, we are prepared to trade with you—crystals if you want or other metals and stones. But to do this we need your help to open the Gate to our realm.'

'So you say.' Lord Hale stared at Danel. 'How can we know your word is true.'

'You can keep the pouch as a sign of our good faith.'

'It is vital that we open the Gate, so we can feed our people before they starve,' Delvina added. 'Our need is dire and urgent.'

'Nevertheless, the company you keep does not induce trust.' Lord Hale waved his sword at Baba, Aunt Bikan and himself.

Zadeki suppressed a growl. Why were the Vaane quibbling? What did they have to lose? Surely it was enough that the Darane were in need. Yet, just as the Tamrin made it more complicated than it needed to be, so too were these people.

'And how is it that the Overseer can't open the Gate to her own realm?' Princess Avardin asked, arching a shapely eyebrow.

'The seal was lost with the previous Overseer, Hezikah's son Uzza, when he fled to the caverns.'

Lord Hale snorted. 'No, no, our need for crystals is not so great that we would negotiate with rebels. What message will that give to the rabble raining havoc on our harbour and attempting to hold us to ransom? It would only encourage the ebed to even greater excesses. Don't you agree Grand Technician?'

The Technician blinked rapidly a couple of times. 'Ah, well, this is a fair point.' He nodded and waved his thin hands at Danel. 'You have your answer. Now go! Leave the island before sunset tomorrow, all of you. Mariner

Habbiah, take them back to Redhaven. I will pen a letter to the Warden Ealam. And then return with more supplies in a timely manner.'

'Your Honour, I entreat you to reconsider,' Danel said.

'We need to open the Gate, sir,' Delvina added.

'Be silent. You have your answer.'

This could not be. Thrown off the island on the briefest of audiences. Only this morning, Aunt Bikan seemed certain of the success of the meeting. Had she and Baba known what the Vaane's reactions would be? Perhaps so, for they'd had a taste of it in Redhaven. Zadeki turned, ready to storm out of this stupid city.

Princess Avardin held up the crystal to the light. 'My dear Iulien, let's not be so hasty. Would it not be wise for the Council to consider all the implications?'

'What can there be to discuss, dear Princess?'

Avardin lifted her shapely chin and met the Grand Technicians impatient gaze. 'Lord Hale's concerns may well be valid as former Minister of Mines and our Overseas Possessions, but his is but one opinion.'

Mariner Habbiah cleared his throat. 'Besides, your Honour, I could not leave the island until the White Rose is adequately repaired from extensive storm damage. It will take half a ten-day to fix it.'

The Grand Technician dropped his gaze. 'Oh, very well. But what is to be done with them in the meantime?' He pushed out his lips, then smirked. 'Master Mariner Habbiah, since you undertook to bring them to our city, you will act as their hosts and take responsibility for their actions.'

'But, your Honour, I was only fulfilling ...'

'Take them to your dwelling and bring them back

here when the Council has made its decision. They are not to shapeshift for any reason, nor stir up trouble. They must stay within the city confines. Lord Hale will assign watchers to keep an eye on them.'

The Master Mariner placed his hands on his chest and bowed. 'As you wish Grand Technician.' He waved at them. 'Come.'

Danel stood like a boulder, legs a stride. 'Our thanks, your Honour. Princess Avardin. We will await your decision.'

Zadeki felt like cheering. The mountain dwellers may be short in statue, but big on courage and grit. Though he wished he knew what was troubling Delvina.

Zadeki followed behind his friends, ignoring the hostile stares of the Vaane. Not the best outcome for the meeting, but at least it was a start.

Delvina hurried to catch up with the long strides of the Mariner and Forest Folk. Even Danel was taller than she. Mariner Habbiah stopped at the bottom of the stairs and subjected them to a sweeping glance.

'I can send for Samwin to bring the cart, if you wait here. You three shapeshifters best stay covered.' He handed them the discarded cloaks.

'It can't be far to walk,' Highwun Korak tugged the hood further over his forehead with a grimace. 'If you have no objection, children of the mountain?'

'Not at all,' Danel said almost before Korak had finished speaking.

Habbiah scrunched his mouth, then shrugged. 'The house is a fair distance, close to the academy in the south. Just try to keep up.'

With that he strode down the street, his cloak flapping in the wind behind him.

Highwun Bikan waved Delvina and Danel on, falling in behind them in a protective semi-circle.

Delvina broke into a jog to match the Mariner's fast pace. Even so, it felt good to stretch her muscles, to feel solid stone beneath her boots, especially as she no longer felt the ground swaying as though she was still on the deck of the White Rose or lurching in the cart for that matter.

The sun had passed the high point in the sky, the pale crescents of golden and silver moons following behind. The streets were less crowded now. Even the Forest Folk drew no more than the occasional curious looks, hidden as they were beneath the hooded cloaks reaching to their ankles. She was glad of it in a way, as it was easier to avoid Zadeki's attempts to start a conversation.

The wonders of this city, which might once have delighted her, now seemed overbearing, full of flourishes and unnecessary ornamentation. Perhaps designed to make her and those like her feel unimportant and to keep them in their assigned places.

After a while, she kept her eyes fixed to the ground. She and Danel may as well have been invisible anyway, as eyes slid over their heads. She had never felt so belittled, even when she and Retza were crewless and scrounging for food in the Commons. And once again, their request, this time for information, was delayed and perhaps denied. If it hadn't been for Princess Avardin's intervention, they would have been sent back to the ship and cast off the island with no answers.

They turned down a small laneway beside a building of white stone and a blue-tiled roof. Mariner Habbiah rapped on a blue door.

After a few moments it opened to reveal a young ebed woman with light brown skin. She bowed and stood aside. 'Glad to see you back, sir.'

'As you say. Inform your mistress we have arrived, Irina.' He swept off his short cloak and threw it at the ebed, before beckoning Delvina and the others to enter into the small hallway. The watchers remained outside the door.

Irina reached out to take hold of Highwun Korak's cloak at the same moment he slipped it off his shoulders. Their hands met, and Irina jumped backward, her red-brown eyes widening.

'I beg your pardon, sir.' Her tan cheeks flushed.

Highwun Korak gave a reassuring smile. 'No matter, child.'

Habbiah seemed not to notice. 'Did my daughter arrive safely, Irina?'

'Yes, sir. She is directing the preparation of the meal.' Irina took the cloaks from Bikan and Zadeki, but took no notice of Delvina or Danel.

'Ah, good, good. These travellers will be staying for a few days at least, maybe longer. If you can see accommodation prepared—and please, be discrete about our guests.' Habbiah waved a hand toward a beaded doorway. 'This way, gentle Bikan, Korak.'

He brought them into a paved courtyard, Delvina and Danel following the others. A carved fountain stood at the centre, its melodic tinkle soothing. Rooms partially screened with vines, flowering plants and decorated partitions opened off the area on all sides. A sky laced with grey clouds formed the ceiling above their heads. Small birds trilled in the bushes. Pretty, though Delvina would have preferred solid walls and a roof.

Zadeki spun around on one spot, dark eyes drinking in the details. 'This I like. Less stone, more green.'

'Make yourself comfortable.' Habbiah indicated some low-set stools and cushions scattered on a woven mat. 'Ariel will join you soon. Early tomorrow, I'll need to get back to Destruction Bay to ensure the ship has been unloaded and supervise the repairs. I will leave Samwin at your service. Excuse me while I arrange to necessary details.' The Mariner strode away toward the front of the dwelling.

'So glad to get out from under that wretched cloak,' Zadeki muttered, scratching his neck.

Highwun Korak remained standing. 'Should I scout the area, father's sister? Look for escape routes or possible threats?'

Bikan settled down on a cushion, sighing. 'As tempting as it is brother's son, we best not upset our hosts. No shapeshifting for now.' She yawned and leaned back against a carved divider. I'm getting too old for this.'

Delvina sighed and sat on a bright red cushion with a bird design embroidered on it. She sank down into it, its softness somewhat disconcerting. Danel perched on a stool next to her, his eyes huge as he studied the open space and the roofline.

Zadeki circled the courtyard, tracing with strong fingers the images formed by gold, silver and gemstones inlaid into wood lacquered red and black. He picked up a glazed pot and then put it back. Stroked the leaves of a potted tree, his eyes alight with curiosity.

'Sit down, youngling,' Highwun Bikan waved a hand.

'Yes, father's sister.' He jumped up and balanced on a high bench with one leg swinging.

Delvina's eyelids wanted to close, though the events

of the last day or so circled in her mind. So much had happened, so much had changed.

Moments later, Irina returned with other ebed carrying enamelled trays loaded with dishes of food—fish and rolls like they'd had for breakfast, cheeses, fruit of various kinds, greens and other vegetables in rich sauces, pickled eggs, small roasted birds, and other delights. They placed them on low tables along with plates, napkins and bowls filled with scented water.

Irina shot Delvina and Danel a pointed look. She moved in front of Highwun Bikan and bowed. 'Do you wish your ebed to serve you, Gentle?'

Bikan sat up straight, a small frown creased between her dark eyebrows. 'They are our companions, child.'

Irina's face paled. 'Forgive my assumption. If you indicate your preferences ...'

Bikan waved her away. 'No, no, we can serve ourselves.'

Korak placed his hands on his chest and bowed his head. 'We thank you for providing us with such bounty, but we won't keep you from your other tasks.'

'As you wish Gentles.' She backed out of the room and the other ebed followed.

Delvina and the others crowded around the platters, loading up food on the plates provided.

'What is this,' Danel asked, prodding a strange-looking creature with eight legs and two front claws a little like a cavecray.

'Crab,' Bikan answered. 'River crab is delicious, I'm sure these are too.'

Zadeki found his perch and focused on the mound of food on his plate with a steady dedication.

Delvina stepped toward him, then stepped back to sit

beside Thirdwun Danel, whose plate was piled almost as high.

'This place is amazing. I could never have imagined such wonders.' Following Korak's example, Danel cracked open the crab's leg and sucked out the flesh.

The food, the buildings, it was all amazing, yet Delvina couldn't shake the lethargy that hung like a cloud of bad air around her. 'I wonder how Retza, Overseer Havilah and the others are coping. Perhaps they have managed to clear the tunnels. Maybe the seal will not be needed.'

Danel sobered. 'By the powers that be, one hopes so. But our cause is not lost yet, Runner Delvina.'

'The Grand Technician seems set against us. And Lord Hale too.'

'It is not like you to give up so easily, Delvina.' Danel touched her hand, then sat back suddenly, his cheeks flushing pink. He cleared his throat. 'Princess Avardin at least spoke on our behalf.'

'If you do have access to glimmer crystals, that's a strong bargaining point, though strange that Avardin is supporting you.' Ariel walked into the courtyard, her honey-brown hair cascading over her shoulder and down her back. 'My father has put you into my care. If you need anything, please ask, and I will attempt to accommodate you.'

Danel stood and pulled his beard. 'May I ask, why you find the Princess' support strange?'

'Her father, the King Oban's younger brother, accumulated a great store of the stones and since the closure of the mines, has been able to command a high price for them.'

'Perhaps, the stores are diminishing, and she wishes to replenish them.'

'This is possible. You may be able to do a deal with her, in return for her advocacy with the Council.'

'Even if she is inclined to and the Council agrees, we still do not know if they can do anything with the seal.' Delvina said.

Zadeki rubbed his stomach. 'Perhaps we can do some investigating while we wait, or is that forbidden too?' He glanced first at the Mariner's daughter, then at Highwun Bikan.

Ariel's gaze lingered a little longer on Zadeki's lithe figure. She moved closer to him and placed a soft hand on his arm. 'My father said nothing against it, as long as you remained cloaked in public, refrain from shapeshifting and stay within the confines of the city.'

Delvina bit her lip, and turned towards Highwun Bikan. 'But what can we do?'

'Tonight we should rest. We've all been through a lot. On the morrow, Korak and I will speak to the crystal singers in the craft district. They may know something useful. It might be best if you three younglings stay indoors.'

Zadeki groaned. 'Can't we at least explore the city, father's sister? We'd be careful.'

'Not a good idea, Jazadek,' Highwun Korak said. 'You need to protect our mountain dwelling friends while we're gone, not lead them into trouble.'

Delvina frowned. The prospect of sitting around waiting for an answer reminded her unpleasantly of their stay in Tarka. Like Zadeki, she wanted to do something.

'I know!' Ariel hit her forehead. 'I could take you to the library. There would be something on seals there, for sure. Do you have any objections, Gentle Bikan?'

'Please,' Delvina added her own pleas.

Danel sat up straighter. 'I think we should do it. The more tunnels we explore, the better.'

'As you wish, but make sure these two risk-takers walk straight there and straight back and keep out of trouble.'

Danel laughed. 'I'll do my best, but you know—.'

'Hey!' Delvina threw a cushion at him, then blushed at her unruly behaviour. 'Sorry, Thirdwun.'

He threw the cushion back. 'Not a good start,' he joked.

Delvina grinned. The more she thought about searching the library for answers, the more she liked the idea. It could actually work!

Zara shifted back on the stool, stretching her cramped hand. She dropped the pen, stood up and took a turn around the modified storeroom. This new room was bigger than the last tiny cell, yet she still missed the size of the Heart Room, if not the drafts. Maybe even missed the old woman, Scrybe Barekia, tinkering around the Crystal Heart. She had only Jesson to talk to, and as much as she loved her brother, there was a limit on what they could converse about.

Her stomach gave a loud rumble. Rations were even scarcer if possible and she never felt truly full.

The gong for change of shift clanged insistently.

Jesson's eyes brightened. He sat straighter. He licked his lips and his eyes drifted to the door. 'What do you think we'll have for dinner, Zuzu?'

'What we've had every other time for the last several days.' Mushroom gruel and half an algae cake each. Both her and Jesson's clothes hung more loosely and she'd had to ask the watchers for a piece of rope to keep his breeches up. Clearly, Gilarth was not joking about the realm running out of food. Unless they were the only ones on a starvation diet. Yet all the watchers, Gilarth included, seemed hollow-cheeked and drawn.

Jesson picked up his spoon and hammered the table with it, metal on stone. 'I hope Retza brings our food. We haven't seen him for days.'

He seemed to have forgotten Gilarth's news that the young watcher was caught in the second cave-in. The image of Retza appeared in her mind's eye. She shivered and wrapped her arms tight around her chest at the thought of his body broken and buried beneath tons of rock.

Everything that had happened since Havilah defied Baba was a nightmare she couldn't wake from; their world turned upside down, Baba and her family gone, the deaths, the darkness, the lack of food. How could she tell Jesson his favourite watcher was likely dead? Retza and Delvina were different from the others. She'd seen how the other watchers looked askance at her and Jesson. Uzza's brats, they called them. But Retza wasn't like that. When the Crystal Heart had flooded back to life in the Heart Room, it seemed they might be friends. But it was better she didn't get attached. It kept the lines between them clearly drawn. They were rebels against her father's rightful rule after all. Now Delvina had left the Glittering Realms on some mission and Retza could be dead.

Jesson let the spoon clatter to the table and ran toward her. He tugged at her skirt, his eyes huge with worry. 'Why are you crying, Zara?'

'No reason.' She wiped the moisture from her cheek and hugged her brother tight. She had to face facts. Baba wasn't coming back. And maybe not Retza either. She and Jesson were on their own.

Whatever happened, she must be strong for Jesson to the very end.

Zadeki roused after a night of disturbed dreams and half-wakings at the strange noises beyond the walls of the house. The sound of raised voices in the street, someone running, the clip-clop of horses, the rattle of a cart. He stared at the painted ceiling above him. The patterns of stars and the two moons against a purple-black sky could almost entice him to believe they were real.

He rolled over and stared at the partition that now enclosed sleeping room from the courtyard. A soft pearl-grey light seeped through the transparent fabric. Birdsong welcomed the dawn, both comfortingly familiar yet alien. Softer and less raucous than the vibrant dawn chorus in the Great Forest. A sudden longing for the his woodland home washed over him.

He sat up and stretched muscles aching from the jolting of the cart ride yesterday. The stares of the courtiers and cold welcome hit him again. As beautiful and poised as Silantis was, something about it set his teeth on edge, like eating unripe jelly-fruit. Nothing here was as it seemed.

The others soon stirred and after a more modest early meal, they separated into different parties. The sun was still low in the sky and the shadows long when they filed out into the streets. After a few last-minute instructions and repetitions of old ones, Mariner Habbiah rode off toward Destruction Bay and the White Rose.

Baba clapped Zadeki on the shoulder. 'Be watchful

and avoid trouble. Take good care of our friends.'

'Yes, and you too.'

'The Maker go with you.' Baba pulled the cloak over his head and set off with Aunt Bikan and Samwin to the craft district in the north of the city. The two watchers peeled off and trailed after them.

Ariel watched them go, a crease between her pretty eyebrows.

'Where is this library, then? Is it far?' Delvina asked, her voice unusually harsh.

She had a despondent air. Zadeki flashed a smile at her, but she looked away.

'At the back of the Star Council House. Come, let's go.'

Without the crowds, it didn't take so long to walk. Younglings ran along the street and some ebed had makeshift shelters and cooking fires in the laneways. Refugees from the conflict in the east.

Ariel pulled her cloak tighter around her neat shoulders. 'Samwin says most of the refugees are from White Haven and Safety Bay. Others come from the countryside. Many are camping in the outskirts of the city, that is, if family have no room for them or they don't have a house in town,' she said.

'So, you have more than one house? One in Silantis and one at Redhaven?' Danel asked.

'No, we've been living in Redhaven some time now, but our cousin is happy to accommodate us while we're here.'

Zadeki shrugged. He didn't particularly mind where they slept, though he couldn't shake the feeling that someone watched them from the shadows. The back of his neck itched all the way from the house to the main ceremonial buildings at the centre of the city.

They passed the old shrine shrouded in the shadow of the massive Council building. A cloaked figure swept the steps while another threw seeds for the pigeons and finches that pecked around the old colonnaded building. Ariel turned down the gloomy laneway between the shrine and the Council building. The library stood in a courtyard at the back, narrower but taller than the other two. A flight of narrow stairs led into an entrance hall.

Delvina tilted her head to look up at the seven levels, 'Does the library have its own building? She asked, awe colouring her resonant voice. 'We have a records room. Nothing like this.'

It was impressive, Zadeki had to admit, though he'd prefer to spend the day free of enclosed walls. He missed the Forest.

'Yes, this was built by the second Sea Dragon King, Lexian. It is connected to the most ancient speaking tower.' Ariel started up the stairs.

Zadeki frowned. 'That was not what my Kin say. King Karin, son of Rahim—'

'Don't say that,' Ariel hissed, her eyes widening in horror. 'Those are Flame-get lies and repeating them will get you in trouble. Besides, the children of Starshine were a rabble before the first Sea Dragon King took the throne.'

Zadeki's skin crawled under the heavy woollen fabric of his robe. 'Our songs tell it differently.'

'Then they are wrong.' Ariel stopped and stared at him. 'Everyone knows you Flame-get live in the wilderness without houses or any cities, no better than wild beasts. Posers and pretenders. So how could your ancestors have built anything of note?'

Zadeki's cheeks flushed hot with anger. Though there was truth to her words, it ignored the fact that Doryn and her Kin had been forced from the Lonely Isles by the Sea Dragon King to make a new life for themselves. And a good life at that. He bit down on the first hot words. Getting in a fight with Ariel wasn't what Baba and Aunt Bikan had in mind when they said, 'Stay out of trouble'.

Del stared at the floor, a strange noncommittal look on her normally open face.

Danel tugged his brown beard. 'Those are harsh words, Lady Ariel. Of all the peoples we have met, the Forest Folk are the most generous and humane. We owe them a great deal.'

Zadeki's muscles uncoiled at the unexpected defence. Perhaps it did not matter what the Vaane thought of them, with friends like Danel.

'We are here to investigate the library, not squabble like younglings. Perhaps we should focus on that.' Zadeki gave a lopsided grin.

Ariel tilted her head, her fingers brushing the crystal pendant on her chest. She let out a soft sigh. 'I am a techwun and not nobility, Danel. So "gentle" will do. Son of Korak, please forgive me for my rash speech. You are our guests and ... cannot be blamed for your ignorance.'

Zadeki bristled again, and almost snapped back he wasn't the ignorant one. The stories he'd been taught were different from hers, but of course the followers of the Sea Dragon King would not acknowledge the achievements of their predecessors or their wrong actions against them. She only knew what she'd been taught. 'Please, daughter of the waves and storm, lead the way.'

Ariel's sculpted lips tightened, but with a sharp nod, she led them up the stairs.

A single watcher stood at the door to the building.

The mariner's daughter stepped up and showed him a crystal token. He stood aside and waved them on with barely a glance at Zadeki or the two Darane.

They stepped through the arched entrance into a large round room. Pale morning sunshine flooded through a round skylight, illuminating a circular desk on a large podium at the centre of the room. Seven wide balconies curved around the walls, stacked one on top of the other. It reminded Zadeki of an iridescent shell.

'Seven rooms on seven floors,' Ariel said, with a quick glance over her elegant shoulder. She gave him a tentative smile before approaching the curved desk, where she picked up a golden bell and shook it. A resonant sound tinkled through the circular room. Folding her arms, she stood back and waited.

Somewhere nearby, came a regular drip, drip of water on stone. 'Is there a leak?' Zadeki whispered at last.

Surprise, then disdain flickered over Ariel's sculptured face before she assumed a smile. 'Water clock,' she said. 'It's an old mechanism, not really needed these days with crystal timekeepers, but the library keeps artefacts as well as codices and scrolls. What do you use to measure time?'

'Glimmer clocks,' Danel said.

'The sun, stars and moons, the song of the Forest and the skies,' Zadeki said, then felt foolish as three sets of eyes, one dark, two grey stared at him.

Ariel laughed and was about to say something, when a tall, thin man in silver robes appeared from behind the high partition beyond the desk. He wore a pair of lenses joined by wire over his eyes. 'How can I help, Gentle Ariel?' Like the watchers, he flicked a brief look at Zadeki and didn't even glance at the two Darane.

'We are looking for texts on seal stones, Narrator Kaspin. In particular, if there is any way to transfer ownership or control.'

Uncertainty clouded Kaspin's face. 'You do not plan to use this knowledge unwisely?'

'No, sir. The owner of the seal has passed on without making adequate provision for those who survived him.'

After a long, steady stare, Narrator Kaspin nodded and tented his long, thin fingers. 'I see. Seal stones are, as you should know, soul stones.'

'What are soul stones?' Delvina asked. 'I mean I know the Glimmer Heart is soul-bound but ... but ...' she stuttered as Kaspin's silver eyebrows rose to his hairline.

'Please, if you would explain, Master Narrator,' Ariel rushed to speak.

Kaspin gave Delvina another look from beneath his eyebrows and turned to address Ariel. 'Soul stones are special crystals that can be bound to a particular person or lineage. Once the bond is made, it is difficult to change. The soul stones enhance or amplify ...'

' .... energy sources, like wind and rain and ...' Danel faltered, then continued. '... and the energy in rocks.'

'Indeed, ebed. Are you a technician?' Kaspin radiated irritation like a sizzling pan. 'As I was about to say, more sophisticated soul stones enhance sentient abilities. They enhance the gifts given by the Maker at the dawn of time.'

Ariel nodded and brushed the crystal at her neck with her fingers. 'My farspeaking is much stronger when with my talisman. So, seals are soul stones. I thought they worked through matching the patterns carved into their surface.'

Kaspin inclined his head. 'Many are as you say, mere

rocks that will work for one person as well as for another, but a true seal stone works only for the owner.'

'It is soul-bound.'

'Yes, as I said.'

'And is there any way to transfer the ownership?'

'A provident person establishes the bond or at least a means of transfer with his or her heirs before they pass on to the eternal realms. This is how house seals are passed down from generation to generation.'

Zadeki ran his fingers along the patterns in the wood panelling, each line representing a season of growth. Seiba wood, from the Great Forest most like. The soul bond of the Crystal Heart had passed on to Lady Zara through touch. Perhaps, something similar would work for the seal?

'What if we don't have the seal?' Danel asked.

Kaspin drew himself up, eyebrows bristling. 'Look, if you expect me to get involved in this ebed rebellion against lawful masters, you will be disappointed. I want no part of it.' He clutched the crystal at his neck.

'What, wait!' Ariel cried out.

'We're not with the protest at the harbour,' Zadeki said.

Ariel caught the Narrator's hand. 'It's true. These are visitors to our isle and the Grand Technician has asked my father to host them while he considers their offer for trade.'

'And their ward is in Redhaven?'

'Far from here. In the mountains on the mainland.'

'I suppose, if the Grand Technician has approved.'

Ariel spread out her hands. 'He has not forbidden it. Surely, there are legitimate cases like this one, when the seal is lost with the death of the master or mistress?'

'Humph. Rare, very rare indeed. Who would be so careless. Without the seal itself, I don't think I can help.'

'Could a new seal be made?' Delvina asked.

'Humph, it may be possible but I don't know how. If there are any answers, they'll be in the blue section, six levels up.'

Ariel cupped her hands on her chest and bowed. 'Our thanks for your help. Would you grant us access to blue level, sir?'

Kaspin rubbed his chin. 'The Grand Technician, you say?'

'Yes,' Ariel said, her face as innocent as a new day.

'Very well then, but make sure you supervise your … companions.'

Ariel took the disk and bowed. 'Our thanks.' She beckoned for Zadeki and the others to follow and strode to the spiral stairs.

'Anyone would think we were unruly pets,' Zadeki grumbled.

'Doesn't matter,' Delvina answered. 'As long as we get answers.' She gave him a sad smile. She looked even paler than usual except for her slightly red and flaking nose.

'Are you sure you are up to this, Del'? he asked.

'Yes, of course.' A shadow passed over her face, and she turned away from him. She had not been the same since the shipwreck. But then she'd been a hair's breadth from drowning and was no doubt recovering from a long and tiring journey from the mountains to the Island.

'I don't remember the Grand Technician saying we could use the library,' he said.

'It wasn't among the restrictions.' Ariel gave them a knowing look. 'Are you coming?'

'Come, we better not keep the gentle waiting,' Zadeki whispered.

Danel and Delvina laughed. He grinned back at them and hurried after Ariel. There had to be a way to replace the old Overseer's seal on the Gate. And this was the best place to start their search.'

Delvina put down the scroll and stretched her back. She couldn't believe how much paper there was in this building. Even a small piece cost a week's ration in her underground home. Golden-pink light filtered through the circular skylight, signalling the closing of another day. But for all that, she'd not found anything more than the Narrator had already told them.

'How many scrolls and tomes have we read and still nothing? Found anything of interest, Danel?'

A soft snore answered her. Danel was slouched in the corner, head back and mouth slightly open, an open codex in his slack hands. Perhaps it was time to pack up and head back to the house. She looked around the curve of the sixth level. Dust motes jiggled in beams of sunlight. A sweet scent of old paper mingled with dust and leather.

Further down the aisle, Zadeki and Ariel sat cross-legged on the patterned floor, a heap of codices and scrolls between them and dark heads almost touching. They looked good together, similar heights and colouring.

Delvina swallowed the bitter taste. She barely came up to Zadeki's armpits. She rubbed calloused fingers along the spine of the book. Was she a fool to imagine ... what? A future together? Where would they live? The caverns suffocated him, and while she had craved new sights, would she be able to live in the Great Forest under flimsy shelters that provided fragile protection from the elements? So, it was for the best, wasn't it? But what if ...

'Don't be silly, Delvina,' she muttered to herself. 'It's not about you. This is a distraction.' They had to find answers, or she wouldn't have a home. Her brother Retza, the Overseer Havilah, Scrybe Barekia and all the others would starve. Might already be starving.

She rolled up the scroll, picked up the pile she'd already read and walked back to the stacks.

As she walked past, Ariel fingered Zadeki's hair. 'I thought all Flame-get had red hair.'

Zadeki batted her hand away. 'Some do, but not all of us. And you know, I wish you wouldn't say Flame-get all the time. It's offensive.'

Delvina replaced the first scroll in its niche. 'Like earthbiter,' she muttered, louder than she meant to. Zadeki could hear keener than a bat seeking moths in the dark.

He turned his head toward her, eyebrows shooting up. 'Oh, well. Sorry, Delvina. I won't say it again.'

She pulled at her tunic collar, suddenly hot and stuffy in the clothes Ariel had insisted they wear. 'So you don't stand out. It's our house livery.' So that they looked like ebed, servants, is what she meant.

'Are you alright, Del.' Concern clouded Zadeki's midnight-dark eyes. He stood in one graceful movement.

That was another thing. She clumped along like a broken glimmer truck. How could she compete with someone like Ariel?

Her fingers fumbled, the top scroll tipped, and the others began to slip.

One step and Zadeki caught them before they cascaded to the floor. 'It's been a long day looking at fusty volumes. We can come back tomorrow.'

His fingers brushed hers, sending a shock through her. Tears welled up, blurring his face.

'Don't worry, Del, we'll find a way to bypass the seal. We'll open the Gate and get the food to your people. It's going to be alright.'

She sniffed back the tears and nodded, not sure what to say.

'So, do Flame-ge … Shapeshifters use crystals?' Ariel stood close, her gaze darting from Delvina to Zadeki.

'Why would we?' Zadeki frowned, his voice unusually sharp.

'To shapeshift.'

'No, we don't need to enhance our powers with crystals.' He turned a shoulder to Ariel and slotted a scroll in its niche.

'Because your gift is not from the Maker.'

'What? Yes, of course it is. Where else would it come from?'

'The Shadow Master, father of deceit. It must be why the Sea Dragon King banned your kind.'

'No, that's not true.' Zadeki seemed to swell and Delvina could almost see the jaguar stirring inside him. Why was the silverskin girl baiting him? Was the Shadow Master like the Dark Ones? The thought was ridiculous.

Delvina spun around, her chin thrust out. 'Leave him alone. What's wrong with you? I thought you were meant to be helping us, not insulting us.'

Ariel took a step back, eyes blazing. 'How dare you speak to me like that, why I—'

'I'm not one of your ebed slaves,' Delvina yelled. Just like the old Overseer or his daughter, Lady Zara, thinking themselves better than everyone else.

Zadeki grabbed her shoulders, pulled her back. 'It's

alright, Del.' His breath ruffled her hair, and she could feel the steady rhythm of his heart against her shoulder blades.

Ariel clenched delicate hands, her brown eyes huge. 'They are not slaves. Ebed are retainers and are fairly rewarded for their work. Work they enjoy and are fitted for, passing their skills down the generations.' She sounded shrill.

'If you say so, Gentle.' Danel's voice was calm and kind of gravelly. His brown hair stuck out at different angles and his livery jacket was skewed. 'Though the barricade in your harbour might say otherwise.'

Ariel gasped, her eyes huge. 'Those are rebels.'

'So what are they rebelling against? Not that it's our concern. We are not from around here.'

'Best keep our voices down, we don't want to be thrown out for making a disturbance,' Zadeki said.

Ariel stared at him, a torrent of expressions rushing across her face. After a few moments, she looked down and a soft pink blushed her cheeks. 'My apologies if my words have offended.' She peeked up at Zadeki then looked away. 'Clearly we have been studying, for too long. Let's pack up and go home.'

Zadeki's fingers tightened a second on Delvina's shoulder before he let go. He gave a low laugh. 'Sounds good to me. I'm ravenous.'

Danel rubbed his eyes and yawned. 'I reckon Scyrbe Barekia would give her last tooth for all the information about soul stones, crystals and seals stored here, but we've found nothing that the Narrator hasn't told us already.' He glanced up the tall stacks covering the walls and jutting out into the space. 'It may be here, but it could take for ever to find it.'

Delvina felt the tension ease out of the air.

Danel tilted his head and smiled at her. 'Unless you want to keep going, Messenger Delvina.'

Good, solid Danel. She blinked back sudden tears. She was glad he was here. And Zadeki. 'We need a break. The words were beginning to blur together.' Not to mention tempers fraying. Tomorrow they would come back and the day after that, until they found the answers they sought.

Retza clung to a strut, a little way from the wall of rubble and as far out of the water as he could manage. He drifted in and out of sleep, despite the clamour of the toolwuns' shouts and determined digging on the other side. It was taking longer than he'd thought it would with the collapsed wall thicker than he'd estimated, but at least help was on its way.

It was hard to focus, his mind drifting in and out of awareness. He'd stopped shivering some time ago, though his clothes clung to his wet skin and he could no longer feel his hands or feet. He fought against an overwhelming desire to sleep. At least, the crews knew there were survivors and hopefully they'd reach them in time.

The crash of picks and shovels against rock echoed in the darkness, spelling out hope in discordant notes.

It couldn't hurt to close his eyes until rescuers reached him. His head dropped against his chest and sleep claimed him.

No one spoke as they made their way back to the house. Clouds piled up on the eastern horizon tinged with pinks and orange, and light sparkled inside the houses and supply outlets, or stores as Ariel called them. One bright star shone with a steady glow like a promise of help, and in the greying eastern sky, the two moons one floating above the other.

Danel scuffed his boots along the paved road and trailed behind the others. Were they doing the right thing, making their own investigations? What if the Grand Technician took offense and refused to help them because of it? Should they approach Princess Avardin and ask her to speak on their behalf? The hardest thing was not knowing what was happening. Nebam should have cleared the collapsed tunnel by now and recommenced digging.

'Thanks for speaking up for me, Thirdwun Danel.' Zadeki's face, slightly luminescent in the shadows of his hood, looked more solemn than normal. Ariel strode ahead of them, with Delvina trailing a couple of paces behind.

'These Vaane, they don't seem to like your Kin. Or think too much of my people, either.'

Zadeki shrugged his wide shoulders and made a face. 'We are not here to be loved, but to get answers.'

'We've got few enough of those. If we had the seal and could transfer authority to Overseer Havilah, we could open the Gate.'

'It must be possible. The Regent now controls the seal even though he isn't a close blood relative to the last Sea Dragon King. Besides, maybe we can find a way to override the seal. You can't just break down the Gate with one of those digger trucks of yours?'

'Nebam tried, but there are actually seven gates. Each is booby-trapped. Several toolwuns died before they could even get close to the first one. We need some way to outwit the defences, and I'm not sure we can do that without the Overseer's seal. Nothing I read today came even close to providing solutions.'

'Maybe Aunt Bikan and Baba will be more successful,' Zadeki said.

'I hope so. I wish I understood these people more.'

Delvina stopped suddenly in front of them, her grey eyes wide. 'What is that?'

Up ahead, an ornate framework of wrought bronze stood in the middle of extensive gardens. Its airy dome reached higher than the surrounding trees. From within it came a cacophony of bird calls. A long graceful building stood further back and behind a small lake. Light spilled out from every window, beckoning with promises of food and comfort inside its elegant walls.

Ariel walked back a few paces to them with a toss of her head. 'What is it?'

'Why would they imprison birds?' Zadeki ran a hand through his dark curls, dislodging the cloak's hood. His dark eyes were troubled.

'Oh, that's Princess Avardin's house. She has a reputation as a collector, and has many exotic things brought from the land beyond the oceans, including the birds for her aviary.'

'You mean, our lands.'

'That is disputed.'

Danel intervened before the two could start squabbling again. 'This Heir, could we speak to him directly, rather than go through the Grand Technician?'

Ariel raised her honey-brown eyebrows. 'He is still an infant.'

'If he is so young, why not choose another to be King

or Queen?' Zadeki studied the house and grounds with a crease between his dark eyebrows.

Ariel tossed her hair over her shoulder. 'Doesn't the eldest child of your leader inherit the title of Kinleader?'

'The Elders will choose the one most suited to lead. It may be Elder Bikan or maybe Pathfinder Jasalim, but who knows until the time comes.'

'So, it could be you?' Ariel scoffed.

A burst of laughter escaped Zadeki. 'No, that's not likely. Josenif would make a good Kinleader one day. Not me though. But, by the Maker's favour, Da-Matu—Telsima, Ruhanna's daughter—will lead us for many years to come.'

Ariel snorted. 'Sounds like it could be confusing. What if no one can agree?'

'They would, eventually.'

The two looked set to squabble like siblings. Danel cleared his throat. 'So, Princess Avardin has a lot of influence?'

Ariel turned her back on Zadeki. 'Yes, though the Sea Dragon King designated the Grand Technician as Regent until his son's majority. They were great friends, but even so, it's an unusual choice because Iulien's family have no direct blood ties to the royal house. And the ebed rebellion has eroded confidence in his competency even more.'

'So Grand Technician Iulien cwould be familiar with legitimate ways to override an Overseer's seal? '

'Yes. Though the bigger question is whether the Regent would be willing to share such secrets especially in the current climate.'

'We won't know until we are granted an audience. In the meantime, I think we should keep looking for answers ourselves.' Zadeki threw a pebble along the street.

'Perhaps the others have had better success.' Though Danel wasn't sure what Bikan and Korak hoped to find.

He set off down the road. Walking in the streets of Silantis made him nervous. The sooner they found the answers the better.

Delvina lagged behind the others. Ariel and Zadeki seemed to have made their peace, and Danel was on their heels, his head bowed in thought. As the light bled out of the sky, round lamps lit up along the street, casting pools of light and darkening the shadows. The sounds and smells of food preparation seeped into the street.

She had to get a grip of herself and focus on what was important. The trouble was she missed home, missed her twin, even the simple days of scraping a living on the Commons. True they slept hungry most nights, but before all this began, the weight of saving the realm didn't bear down on her either. Each time the crisis was resolved, another popped up its head.

A sudden commotion erupted in the side street, a loud crashing noise followed by angry shouts. Delvina peered into the unlit laneway. Did someone need help?

She turned to call the others just as they disappeared around the corner. She hadn't realised she'd gotten so far behind. Maybe it wasn't such a great idea to stop.

'Hey, you, ebed. Get over here and help.' The abrasive voice of a sturdy silver-skinned man in tunic and breeches appeared out of the shadows.

'I need to catch up with ...'

'Don't give me sass, girl. I need you.'

The man caught her wrist and pulled. She resisted, planting her feet firmly on the paving stones. Her heart hammered so hard, it felt like thunder.

'Help, Zadeki,' she called, her voice coming out as a squawk. 'Help,' she managed to shout.

The man gave her a shake. 'You ebed are getting above yourselves,' he growled. 'Show some respect and do as you're told or I'll call the watchers on you.'

The sound of a horse trotting down the street bore down on them from the north. More trouble. Delvina shivered as the man continued to pull her. She dug her boots in harder and grabbed hold of a fence post. No one was going to take her without a fight.

'Leave me alone.' She raised her arm to shove the rude fellow away. 'I need to get back to my friends.'

'What seems to be the trouble here?' a cool voice asked. A large horse pawed the ground and snorted while its rider stroked its arched neck. 'Peace, Storm Fury, peace.'

The man swung around. 'What business is it ...' His voice frayed away into the wind. 'Princess Avardin, I did not see you.' He let go of Delvina, cupped his hands on his chest and bowed.

'So it would seem. What is your name, fellow? What appears to be the problem?'

'Er, Esor, bronzesmith in Smelt Street. The wheel broke off. I need help righting my cart and this ebed is refusing to help, my Lady.'

'This ebed is under my protection. I suggest you send for your own ebed to help.'

'That will take ... too long. And an idle ebed is constrained by custom to help when needed. I did not realise she was on an errand for her mistress though.'

Delvina bristled at his tone and the implications of his words. She wasn't an ebed, and even if she was, the man had no right to order her about like a piece of machinery.

'Is anyone injured?' Princess Avardin shifted on her horse, not contradicting the man's assumption.

'No, ma'am, I am alone, but the supplies are needed for our defences against the rebellion, and I do not wish to leave the contents of the cart unguarded.'

'Then I'll send you some men from my household. I suggest you go back to your cart and wait. Help will not be long in coming.'

The man backed away, bowing. 'Thank you, my Lady.'

Delvina rubbed her stinging arm, then jerked her head up at the sound of running footsteps echoing down the street from the south.

Zadeki sprinted towards them, his cloak flying out behind, his hood fallen back on his shoulders. Ariel and Danel followed some paces behind.

'And here are your friends to the rescue. Very gallant,' Princess Avardin's voice was amused.

'My thanks, your Honour, for your help.' Delvina gave the Vaane greeting.

'I'm glad I was close by, little one.'

Delvina licked her lips. 'Could ... could you tell me how the deliberations of the Council on our request are progressing?'

'Ah, you must be patient. We have many matters of great import to discuss, especially in the current crisis, and the Grand Technician dithers on each one.'

'Our mission is of vital importance to us, my Lady.'

'I'll be away on the morrow as I have business in my

properties outside of Silantis, but come see me in a few days' time and you can tell me more.' Avardin lent down and handed Delvina a small object. 'Show this to my doorkeeper.'

'Del, Del, are you alright?' Zadeki's shout boomed down the street, his dark eyes shining in the night lights. He came to a stop, panting, his face scrunched with concern.

So he did care for her. Like a sister. 'Yes, I'm fine.'

'I'll leave you to the protection of your friends. Remember my offer.' With a click of the tongue, Princess Avardin urged her horse forward and she soon disappeared back the way she'd come.

Delvina fingered the small crystal ring nestled in her palm. After a moment, she slipped it into a pocket of her tunic to examine later. The Forest Folk were wary of the lady's help, but it might just be what was needed.

'Retza, Retza.'

Someone called him. A woman. Delvina perhaps? Had he overslept his shift?

He rolled on his side, raising his back as a shield against the insistent voice. Exhaustion rolled through him like a rockfall.

'Retza, wake up.' Someone shook his shoulder.

He rolled into a tighter ball. *Go away! Leave me alone!*

'Come on, lad, wake up,' another growled in his ear. Gilarth.

Bootsteps splashed through water. 'Sir.'

'Yes, what is it, Lead Hand?' Gilarth answered.

'No sign of the other two, sir.'

'Are you certain?' the first voice. Havilah.

What was she doing in the bunk room? Or Gilarth for that matter. Retza grabbed for his blanket. It must have fallen off in the night. It was cold, so cold.

'We've searched five lek down the tunnel. It's flooded all the way down and could cave in at any moment. Should we keep looking?'

'What do you think, Gilarth?'

'The water would have been higher most likely, the current much stronger. I'm sorry your Honour, Nebam and Peta were most likely swept away and drowned. It's a wonder this one survived. I could look.'

A rustling sound. A choked off sigh. 'No, enough lives have been lost,' Havilah whispered.

Retza shook his head from side to side. Realisation seeped into his mind. He was in the tunnel. They were going to give up. 'No, no, no.' The words came out in a croaky whisper.

'Better get him to Scrybe Barekia. And then order the tunnel filled in.' Havilah's voice sounded hollow. 'We'll need to tell the families.'

His eyelids were weighed down with stones. They refused to open. He had to tell them. He fought against the arms that wrapped around his shoulders and knees. 'Alive.'

'Yes, and we're thankful for it,' Gilarth said, lifting him up. 'But stop struggling.'

He opened his eyes and blinked at the brightness of the glimmer lights. 'Nebam, Peta, alive.'

'Retza, how could they be?'

'Greenstone South also.'

'He's delirious. Been exposed to the cold and wet too long,' Gilarth said.

'But what if he's right?' Havilah murmured. 'I've all but lost one son, must I lose both? But to risk more lives … how can I as Overseer?'

Gilarth's arms around Retza tightened, the Head Watcher's face hovering above him looked set, determined. 'Then let me go find them, Havilah.'

'I need you more than ever before, Head Watcher.'

'My second, Timon, is capable and can replace me if something happens.'

'Debatable.' A pause. 'Why would you do this?'

Gilarth's lips tightened. 'You know why.' His head drooped. 'I can't change the past, but this I can do. Neither of us can live with not checking.'

Havilah stilled for a moment, her face unreadable. 'You can't blame yourself …'

'Yes, I can and you surely do. I could have done something to help you, perhaps saved Ozier's life. I didn't. This I can do. Please, Havilah.'

Ozier. The name was familiar. The old Lead Hand, Havilah's mate and father of her sons. Retza shivered. The former Lead Hand had died in the same cave-in as his parents. What did Gilarth have to do with that? Was there more to this than he and Delvina had been told?

'Very well but take care. Don't be rash.' Havilah's voice sounded sharp in contrast to her words.

Gilarth nodded once. He waded through the water to the flatbed truck and laid Retza down on it.

'What did you do?' Retza whispered.

Gilarth grimaced. He stripped off his jacket and wrapped Retza in it. 'That's for the Overseer to tell. How far down are they?'

Why was Gilarth being evasive? Maybe just focusing on the job at hand. 'Just beyond the rescue digs.' He pummelled his brain. How far had he walked in the dark? 'Seven lek, or thereabouts. But the tunnel opens up into a lake. 'Karel and the other survivors are on an island. Here, I'll come with you. Someone should.'

'Don't be foolish, you're suffering exposure.'

Retza pushed himself off the truck and took a step. A burning stake spiked through his knee and he sank into the water with a groan.

Gilarth grabbed Retza's arm and dumped him back on the flatbed. 'Here, make sure he gets to the Scrybe. Seven lek. If I'm not back by second shifts.'

'I'll come with you. My choice, Overseer,' the Lead Hand of Copper East, Izan said.

Gilarth straightened and crossed his arms. 'No nee—'

'Thanks for offering, Lead Hand,' Havilah clapped him on the shoulder. 'If it gets too dangerous, turn back.'

Retza could sense their disbelief. They thought he was deluded or confused of both. At least Gilarth and Izan were going.

He sank back on the flatbed, unable to stop shivering and the tunnel swirled around him. *Help is on the way, Peta, Nebam.* He only hoped it wasn't too late. As he sank bank into the oblivion of sleep.

Five days. The White Rose should be repaired by now and still they were no closer to any answers. Delvina settled on a couch in the courtyard like a weary bird returning to her rest. She rolled her aching shoulders and cracked her back, cramped and aching from sitting in the stacks all day, every day. Today had been no different. They knew ownership of the seal could be transferred, but not how or whether it could be overridden or replaced if lost. Seeing Zadeki and Ariel working together didn't help.

Outside, a strong wind whistled about the building, finding all the cracks. Samwin had rolled the covers over the open courtyard, making it cosier. Highwun Bikan and Korak hadn't returned yet. It was just the library foursome huddling close to the fire crackling in the bronze brazier.

Irritation rolled up inside her, making her restless. 'We're wasting our time here,' she growled. 'We should go back home.'

She missed running messages or swinging a pickaxe. Even working in the cesspits seemed preferable to leafing through dusty codices until the letters ran together in an inky blur and her nose itched with dust. Most of all, she missed her twin, Retza. How many times had she turned to say something to him, to realise anew he wasn't there? Over two ten-days since they'd left the Glittering Realms and still no closer to answers or any idea how her people were faring.

'This is a colossal waste of time.' She slammed down her half-empty food bowl.

Danel looked up, his eyebrows raised. 'That's not like you, Delvina, to give up. The answers must be buried somewhere on this island. Besides, isn't it fascinating, discovering how the crystals work. I've already thought of some improvements we could make to the glimmer trucks.' Enthusiasm lit up Danel's face.

Delvina softened a touch. 'I just want to do something. I'm tired of all the talk, all the pointless searching.' She threw a round, yellow fruit with dimpled skin at Zadeki. 'What about you, abovegrounder?'

He caught it as if by instinct. 'Hey, if I can't say

earthbiter, maybe you shouldn't call me abovegrounder.'

'Sorry.' Delvina flushed.

Zadeki grinned back at her, then shrugged. 'I suppose it's true enough. I'm with you, being shut up inside and not being able to shapeshift is getting stale.' He toyed with the fruit before stripping off its thick peel and popping it into his mouth. His straight nose wrinkled. 'That one's a bit tart. Any sweet cakes left.' He hunted around the courtyard until he found the almost empty tray.

Danel chuckled. 'I've never seen anyone eat so much.'

'And I don't even have the excuse of shapeshifting,' Zadeki said through a mouth full of treats. 'Though Baba reckons I'm still growing.' He sobered. 'Maybe the solution is in front of us and we just can't see it. If seals are soul-bound, then they might work like the Crystal Heart. Zara was able to establish a connection through touch—through her heart's beat.'

Ariel put down a pile of accounts and stretched. 'It's got to be more complicated than that.'

'And it would work only if we have the Overseer's seal,' Delvina added. Had Havilah decided to search for the seal? She hoped so. Though if Nebam could salvage the tunnel, all this wouldn't be necessary.

The sound of voices carried from a side entrance. A few moments later, Highwun Bikan walked into the courtyard with Highwun Korak and Samwin following behind. Bikan slipped back her dark hood, revealing wind-blown hair pearled with salt crystals. Fatigue lined her face. Both Bikan and Korak pulled off their robes and sat down.

Irina appeared from the shadows and set out some more food trays. 'Gentles.' She bowed low.

'Our thanks, Irina,' Highwun Korak said with a smile.

'Have your inquiries met any success?' Danel asked.

Korak swallowed a bite. 'No, only confirming the Narrator's words and your own researches. The situation down at White Haven and the docks is escalating though.'

The tension in the city had intensified. More ebed had joined the barricade and the watchers were getting twitchy.

Danel let out a huge sigh. 'And still no word from the Council.'

'If they leave it much longer, it won't matter,' Delvina grumbled. What if the evident hostility between the Forest Folk and the Vaane was harming their cause. Her fingers stroked Avardin's ring. The highwun would most likely be back in Silantis by now. She could help them, though something in her manner unnerved Delvina.

Outside the wind worried at the shutters and sent the edges of the canvas cover flapping.

Delvina shook her head. 'What is the dispute with the rebel ebed about?' The way the silverskins treated the ebed irritated her, like a splinter digging deeper under a fingernail. If the Forest Folk were right, the ebed were her ancestors. 'Would they help us if the Council refuses to?' she mused aloud.

Ariel's hands flew to her mouth. 'You wouldn't. They wish to destroy us.'

Korak put down his now empty plate and gave Delvina a measured look. 'Their grievances seem to have some merit, even if their tactics are less than ideal.'

Bikan spread her hands. 'There is always more than one side to a story. We find it best not to get involved. Such wholesale and indiscriminate destruction can hardly be a good way to find justice.'

Delvina's ears flamed and she gripped her hands together. 'The ebed are treated with disdain and might as well be slaves. I truly wonder if we are asking the right people.'

Danel looks around. 'Hush, Del, they already suspect us of siding with these rebels. Besides, what would they know about the seal?'

'Zadeki fought with us to depose Uzza.' Delvina fixed her eyes on the young shapeshifter.

He frowned. 'To save the lives of innocents.'

Delvina swung around to Samwin and Irina. 'What do you think?'

Irina flushed, and she shrank back into the shadows. 'I am loyal to my mistress' house.'

Zadeki shook his head. 'Del, don't put them on the spot.'

Samwin stood straighter 'We are not slaves. Gentle Bikan is right, there are genuine grievances. The treatment of our people has worsened over the years with the last Sea Dragon King. This ... this is frustrating, yet most of us would not resort to the violence and extreme actions of the agitators. It is such a small number, but I fear it will bring disaster to all.'

Del didn't want to let it go. 'Don't they fight for better treatment of you all?' Hadn't Uzza and his father Hezikah lorded it over the rest of her people, keeping the best for himself and his family and demanding cruel and useless sacrifices to the Dark Ones? It was only right that he'd been overturned.

'It is true, they ask that ebed be treated better, but such an insurrection will only meet with more force, more crackdowns. And this barricade hurts all of us. It cuts off necessary food and other supplies from the land, making it harder to feed our younglings and elderly.' Samwin swallowed hard. 'I do not trust the leaders in White Haven, and it is said they are influenced by someone from the best families, used for their own purposes.'

'Yes, this I sense,' Highwun Bikan said with a note of certainty. 'There is a shadowy force at work inflaming the situation for their own ends, but it is not yet clear to me who it is.'

'That's only rumour,' Irina said, her voice overloud, her cheeks darkening further. 'The rebels are few and will soon be subdued, though the Grand Technician's inaction isn't helping.'

Ariel closed her mouth with a snap. She caught her hands together and breathed out heavily through her delicate nose. 'Samwin, are you unhappy in my father's service. Haven't we treated you well?'

Samwin stiffened, as though he had forgotten Ariel was eating with them. 'Yes, of course, Gentle. Please excuse my rash words.' He bowed and backed out of the room.

Ariel fiddled with her pendant. 'See, you are strangers here and don't understand our ways. It is ill of you to repay our hospitality by stirring up contention among our ebed.'

Delvina snorted. Why couldn't Ariel see what had become so obvious to her? 'What else could he say, since he and all the ebed are confined to a subservient role and are dependent on your favour.'

'It's only natural. You speak of roles, but this is how the Maker has ordained it. A chain of being from the most superior to the inferior, each suited for their position and tasks in life.' Ariel forehead's wrinkled and she picked up the tray and put it down again.

Highwun Bikan shook her head. 'That is not how we see it. The ancient scrolls ...'

Heat rose like a furnace inside Delvina's throat, choking her. It was beyond aggravating. All the insults and slights of the past few days. 'I ... I need some fresh air.' She stood and rushed from the courtyard to the side door, out into the blustery evening.

The watchers at the door did not stop her. In fact they didn't even look at her in her household livery. No doubt she was just another faceless ebed doing her master's errands. She'd stay close to the house and avoid any who might force her labour again.

In the east, the dark column of smoke stood out against the indigo horizon. Dark clouds raced like tattered banners across the faces of the full silver moon and, higher in the eastern sky, the misshapen golden moon. In the west the last remains of the sky bled rusty reds and sulphurous yellows matching her mood.

A wind picked up, lifting her cloak and sending shivers down her back. She wiped the tears from her cheeks. She should have stayed in the tunnels with Retza. Nebam may have cleared the tunnels already, then maybe not. Either way, whether in life or death, she would be with her brother and not among strangers she didn't understand. Not that Zadeki was a stranger. She crushed the thought and walked along the darkened street.

Boots clattered on the paved road behind her. Another ebed on an errand. She shivered. She should go back.

'Delvina, wait up.' Zadeki caught up with her, Danel puffing not far behind.

'I'm not going back, if that's what you want.'

'She's wrong, you know. We are all children of the Maker, all made in his image.'

'Whatever.' Fine words, but he still preferred the Mariner's daughter to her. No, that was unfair. A low band of pressure, like a vice, pressed against her head. Her chest squeezed tight.

'We have to keep trying, Del. Even if we don't find the answer, at least we've tried out best.'

Delvina sighed. 'I know.' She tucked her hands into the pockets of her tunic. The sharp edge of Avardin's crystal ring brushed against her hand.

They walked along the road that led up a hill, each of them lost in their thoughts. Stars winked into existence, bright lights mocking with false offers of hope.

'I'm tired,' she sighed.

'Why don't you rest tomorrow, Runner Delvina. We can continue the search.'

'Are you sure?'

Danel patted her on the shoulder and nodded.

It would mean Zadeki would spend more time with Ariel, but it would also give her an opportunity to take Princess Avardin up on her invitation. If she could only explain how dire her people's situation was, the highborn lady could persuade the Council and the Regent to help them. If anyone could override the Overseer's seal, it had to be the Grand Technician.

She turned back to Habbiah's cousin's house, a new determination in her step. If fate wasn't favourable, she'd make her own fate.

A gong sounded in the distance. Persistent and penetrating. As though calling him to do something.

Retza groaned and pulled the covers over his head. Second Shift. Had he slept in? Did he need to be somewhere? He expected to hear the rustle of watchers rolling out of their bunks, using the ablutions room, pulling on watcher leather, stumping out into the common room to eat.

Nothing. The gong faded into silence. Where was he?

Retza cracked his eyes open to the soft blue dimness of muted glimmerlight. A comfy mattress beneath but no bunk above. He sat up and looked around wildly.

Where was he? Not in the dark, damp tunnels of the cave-in. Not in the Heart Room. Not in any of the dormitories of the watchers, messengers or Greenstone South crew. Not in the Commons or creche.

The room was smallish, with a bed, shelving, desk, and a metal chest for belongings. A few personal things but mostly just necessities.

'Ah, so you're awake at last.' Old Scrybe Barekia stood hunched in the doorway. She shook her walking stick at him.

He pulled the bedcovers up to his neck, suddenly aware he was in his underthings. 'What? How long have I been here?'

'You've slept five shifts away. Wait a minute and I'll get you something to eat and some clothes.' She chuckled.

As if conjured by her words, gnawing hunger awoke in his belly.

Barekia disappeared and came back with a tray loaded with a few shreds of dried fish, some mushroom soup and a softened algae cake sprinkled with fernroot. She placed it on the small chest beside him.

His mouth watered and his hands shook as he shoved the food in his mouth.

'Slow down, slow down,' Barekia scolded, though her wrinkled face broke into a grin.

'Why the extra rations,' he asked, swallowing the fish.

'You've earnt it, young watcher.'

Then it all came tumbling back. The rescue attempts, the second cave-in, the flooded tunnels. 'Peta, Nebam, the others, they're alive. Did Gilarth find them?'

He struggled to stand up, his heading spinning and pain shooting through his knee.

'Not so fast.' Barekia placed knotted fingers on his chest and pushed him down. She was surprisingly strong for a short oldwun over two hundred years. 'To answer your questions. Thank the Maker, yes, Gilarth and Lead Hand Izan found them. It took some figuring out, but they got them across the deep water of the lake. Young Gilarth is nothing if not resourceful. Like his baba in that respect.'

Only Barekia could call Gilarth young. Or maybe the Forest Folk. 'Then, they are ...'

'Doing alright. Nebam has a nasty bump on his head and a broken wrist. A few injuries among the Greenstone South crew, but nothing too serious. And apart from that, lack of food and exposure to the cold and dark. They're going to survive.'

Retza leaned back in the bed. 'It's amazing.' He frowned, 'Who didn't make it?' Surely some didn't survive after being trapped for almost two ten-days, a cave-in and the flooding of the tunnels.

'Here's the thing. They were in the glimmer trucks when the side wall collapsed under the weight of the water. It swept the trucks into the lake, but only a few overturned. They ended up on this outcrop jutting up out of the lake. They didn't have much food between them, but enough to sustain them just and plenty of water. Hard to believe,' Barekia shrugged. 'But there it is.'

Retza's cheeks tugged as an unbidden smile stretched long-forgotten muscles. 'A good sign.'

Barekia nodded. 'And we need it.'

He looked about the room and frowned. 'Where am I?'

'Havilah's room. Thought we better keep an eye on you, young Retza. We were worried there for a while.' She waved a finger at him. 'Now leave your questions for later and eat up.'

For the moment, he was content to do just that.

The mansion reared over her like a dazzling white cliff or a cresting storm wave. Something of the design reminded her of the palace in Tarka, with arched casement windows, balconies, and a tiled roof of brilliant cobalt-blue. Though this building was finer in its lines, more graceful, like a tall silverskin compared to a stocky toolwun. Delvina caught her lower lip between her teeth. Perhaps this wasn't such a good idea.

Her legs slowed as though they had a will of their own. It wasn't too late to join the others in the library.

'Ah, Delvina, what a delight to see you.' The beautiful Princess Avardin strolled from behind a fountain, carrying a bunch of newly picked flowers. Her eyes sparkled and her hair, loosely caught up, gleamed in the sunlight. She was as tall as Zadeki, though more shapely. 'I'd begun to despair of your coming.'

'Gentle.' Delvina gave an awkward bow. 'Please pardon my intrusion, but I remembered your kind invitation.' Her voice faltered.

Princess Avardin inclined her head. 'And I am glad

you did at last. But come, let's get out of the sun. The day is already heating up.' She waved toward the aviary, with its curved and ornate metal-like white lacework. Avardin led Delvina through the fretwork gate into a small forest with delicate flowers cascading from trunks and branches.

It was like an enchanted version of the Great Forest, tamed and contained in a giant cage and somehow transported to the Lonely Isles. Frothy foliage fluttered in the soft breeze. Rainbow butterflies and birds with brilliant plumage flittered among the branches. Floral aromas mixed with the smell of wet leaves and soil. The soft tinkle of water and small rustlings in the undergrowth added to the illusion. Yet, here she didn't feel exposed to the sky and its unpredictable elements.

'Delightful,' Delvina breathed.

'I'm glad you like it,' Princess Avardin said. 'Come this way, my sweet.' The gracious lady seemed to glide down a winding path to a clearing set with a round white filigree table and two chairs. An ebed, a young girl with skin of light ivory and dressed in pretty robes, stood to the side with a tray of refreshments; delicate fruit confections, small tarts, honey cakes and sugared nuts, and two tall frosted glasses of a light green drink.

Delvina shivered. It was almost as if she were expected.

'Place the tray on the table, Maia, my dear.' Princess Avardin pulled out the nearest chair. 'Please, Gentle Delvina, sit, eat, enjoy.'

'Oh, I'm not a gentle.' Delvina dipped her head to hide her confusion. She wasn't an ebed, a servant, either. She accepted a tart filled with a deep red fruit and perched on the edge of the seat, wishing her feet could reach the moss-carpeted ground. She felt caught in a dream. Avardin was the first Vaane with silver skin to treat her as though she were a person of value. The princess was unlike sturdy, dependable Havilah or even lithe Telsima. Glamorous, beautiful, stately—she exuded power and charisma. 'I'm honoured by your kindness, my Lady.'

She nibbled the pastry, flavour bursting inside her mouth. Another bite and it was gone.

Princess Avardin waved an elegant hand and smiled. 'I am glad you came. Tell me, are you enjoying your stay in Silantis? What do you think of our city?'

'I haven't seen anything like it. It is so beautiful.' Delvina looked at her hands resting in her lap, scarred and calloused. 'How soon before the Council gives us an answer.'

'Ah,' the Princess swirled her glass and raised it to perfect dusty pink lips. She took a delicate sip. 'I'm distressed to say, it could take many days.'

'But that will be too late!'

'Has your own search for answers proved fruitful?'

Ice spiked down Delvina spine. She opened her mouth to speak. What should she say to the lady? How much did Avardin know? Were they supposed to be searching? Could she trust her? Both Highwun Bikan and Zadeki had warned her to be wary of Avardin's motives. The image of Ariel leaning over Zadeki, alternatively teasing him and courting his attention rose to her mind. She squashed it down. What did the Forest Folk know? They didn't use technology, didn't build houses, didn't store knowledge that she could see. They seemed like children, naïve and uncultured, compared to the Vaane. Though they treated you with respect, a small voice said.

She looked up into Avardin's brilliant, multicoloured eyes, blues, greens and honeyed amber, sparkling with amusement.

The Princess waved a finger, as though scolding a recalcitrant littlewun. 'The Grand Technician would not be pleased if he heard you were accessing the library.'

Delvina couldn't pull her gaze away. 'I ... that is we ...' Would they be thrown off the island in disgrace or worse. 'We need to know. Our people will starve if we can't open the Gate.'

In a cloud of sweet perfume, Avardin leant across the table and placed her hand over Delvina's. 'Do not be concerned, sweet Delvina. I understand your urgency even if others on the council like Iu ... others don't. Your secrets are safe with me. Have you found anything of note?'

Delvina started to say, 'Nothing, really.' Instead, she found herself spilling it all out; the long days of fruitless research in the library, her concerns for her brother, Havilah and the others, even her one-sided feelings for Zadeki and annoyance at Ariel's interest in the young shapeshifter, the slights she felt at being accosted in the street or ignored. Once she started, she couldn't stop. Avardin responded with sympathetic noises and words of understanding. It was as though the words were pulled out of her despite her better judgement. Though it felt good to unburden herself to one who listened so well, who sympathised with her predicament. With each word, she could feel the burden that had pressed down on her day after day lifting.

'... And then she said we were inferior beings. As ... as though we were all arranged like different grades of ore.' Delvina frowned, perhaps Avardin believed this too, but surely not when she seemed so generous and kind.

Princess Avardin tapped long fingers on the table. 'Many Vaane believe this to be true.' She offered the plate. 'Have another treat.'

Delvina ignored the offer. 'Do you?'

'Oh no, such babblings are for the insecure.'

Delvina sat back on the chair and fanned her face, suddenly unsure of herself. Had she said too much? Golden sunlight showered down through the interlacing green of leaves. All around her birds trilled musical arias.

'Will you help us?' she asked. 'Do you know how we can open the Gate with or without the seal?'

Princess Avardin lifted a delicate shoulder. 'There is always a key in transferring ownership of a seal. My uncle, the late Sea Dragon King ... ' she stopped. 'The Monarch or his representative, his Regent, would have a master seal that would override the one possessed by the Overseer of the Mines, this Uzza you speak of, that is, if it hasn't been discarded following the closure of the mines. There would also be a key, some way to transfer the soul-bond of the seal to Uzza's heir in case of sudden death. The trick is in discovering what it is.'

'So the Prince ... would he help?'

'He is but a child, a babe in arms. Such a shame that his father and mother were killed last year in a tragic accident just like his grandfather. The Grand Technician would have access to the master seal.' Avardin flicked a bug off the table. 'And your guides, the Adelphi. Have they been frequenting the library with you?'

'No, just Zadeki. They've been making enquiries among the crystal singers and ...' Delvina rubbed her forehead, suddenly aware of a small throbbing pain. What had Bikan and Korak been doing over the last six days? They hadn't said.

Avardin's lips thinned. 'You should be wary of our wayward brethren. They are masters of deceit. How can you trust creatures that change shape at will?'

'Oh, I don't think ... They have been so kind and helpful.' The Forest Folk's shapeshifting was a bit unnerving, Bikan a touch intimidating, but she couldn't imagine Zadeki or Korak deceiving her.

'Their intentions may be honourable, but I'm concerned they may be using you. Ever since they were banished, they've been seeking a way back onto the island.'

Delvina gulped down the last drops of the cool minty drink, so unlike anything she'd tasted before, and wished for more. Why hadn't Bikan and Korak joined their searches in the library? It wouldn't take so long to find answers from these crystal singers.

'Are you sure you've found nothing?'

Delvina jerked her head up. 'No, I mean yes.' Singing. For the Forest Folk the rhythms of life were like songs. Patterns, connections, vibrations. How had the verse gone? '*To the chosen shepherd attune, to red heart's beat vibrating, and in true seed's crimson ikor replenished.*' She'd made the connection between the verse, the old Overseer's daughter's heartbeat and the Crystal Heart. Was there a similar connection between the seal and its soul-bond? But how? 'Songs are vibrations of sorts,' she murmured.

'What did you say?' Avardin leant forward, her eyes suddenly intense.

'Oh, just something from Barekia's manual.' Delvina fought against the overwhelming craving to sleep.

In the distance, a bee buzzed, and birds chirped with midday sleepiness. Why was she so tired? It wasn't midday yet. Though so much had happened over the last several rosters, being chosen as a sacrifice, the fight at the Sunken Temple, the trek across the top of the world to find Zadeki and the Forest Folk, Putarn's rebellion, the death of so many, the fight with Retza, dear Retza, the trip to Tarka and then Redhaven and the Lonely Isles, the storm, almost drowning, the long days of fruitless search through dusty tomes. One event after the other, until she had no time to think. No wonder she was weary.

Avardin's cool fingers brushed her arm. 'Focus, sweet Delvina. Just for a few moments longer.'

Her heart thudded against her ribs. Heartbeat vibrating. 'Patterns. Patterns of vibrations like a heartbeat, or ... or ... a song ... or'

'A song. Yes, or perhaps words or music. You could be right. Something to think about.'

Princess Avardin's face blurred. Delvina took a deep breath and sat up straighter. Was that it? A song or special words to confirm ownership of the seal. But they still didn't have the seal, did they? 'I should go back.'

'No, no. You don't look well. Rest a while and then I'll order the carriage to take you back where you are staying. Here, let me help you.'

'Thanks, but I'll be fine.'

Avardin took her arm, pulled her to her feet, guided her through the riot of colours in the aviary. They stepped through the gate and Delvina blinked at the full blast of the sunlight. In the distance, thunder rumbled on and on, though the sky was a hard, brilliant blue.

Delvina swallowed. The thought of walking through the dazzling stone streets in the full light of day, seemed more impossible by the minute. 'Maybe the carriage.'

'Yes, come to the house and wait in the cool of the

hall. And thank you, Delvina, I've really appreciated our talk. You've been most helpful.'

The words of the codex blurred and danced on the yellowed page. Zadeki rubbed his eyes and sat back against the wall, feeling the stacks close in around him. He tapped his fingers on the floor and shifted position. He couldn't stop thinking about Delvina's outburst and her decision not to join them today. Ever since they'd arrived in Silantis, she'd been acting strangely—distant, snappish, contrary—and he couldn't put his finger on the cause. It was like an itch just out of reach.

'Really, Zadeki, you're as restless as a cat on sun-baked tiles.' Ariel put down the scroll on the desk in front of her. 'What's got into you?'

He shook his head, not sure how to answer. It wasn't just Delvina. His skin prickled with tension, as if caught in the build-up and breathless pause before a thunderstorm in the Forest. The sensation was only getting worse. And though he kept checking through the windows, the sky outside was a brilliant blue, with not a cloud visible. He closed the codex and ran a finger over the embossed cover.

'Well?' Ariel persisted. 'Are you sickening with something?'

'No,' he shrugged. 'I'm worried about Delvina.'

Ariel's sliver-white face seemed to darken. 'I'm not sure what got her so excited last evening.'

'Many things, no doubt.' Zadeki glared at the Mariner's daughter. 'All that stuff about superior and inferior beings, for instance.'

She had the grace to blush. 'It's what the scrolls say.'

'No, they don't. Vaane, Darane, Tamrin—we are all valued by the Maker, all his children.'

'And do you have sacred scrolls in the Forest?'

'Yes, we do. Just because we don't build stone ...' tombs he almost said. '... houses, doesn't mean we're illiterate. Delvina doesn't seem herself.'

'Not since the shipwreck,' Danel affirmed. He blew air out of puffed cheeks. 'We're not finding anything new, or maybe we've found it and didn't recognise it. Let's go back to the house and see how she is.'

'Good idea.' Zadeki jumped up, wasting no time in returning the dusty scrolls and codices to their niches.

'If that's what you want,' Ariel grumped. 'I could use a break. This is not how I was planning to spend my time in Silantis.'

They hurried down the stairs and out the door into the bright sunlight. The old Temple stood in front of them drowsing in midday heat. Low rumbling booms rolled in from the direction of White Haven. Zadeki was surprised not to see thick, black thunderheads roiling on the horizon, though the smoke still poured into the sky and danger scented the air. Something definitely wasn't right.

He pulled the hood over his head, stifling as it was, and strode down the laneway, fighting the urge to run, to shapeshift and find Delvina as fast as he could.

'Wait up,' Ariel ran a few steps to catch up with him. 'You're leaving your friends behind, longlegs.'

Danel jogged behind her, red-faced and puffing. 'Don't mind me.'

'Sorry.' Zadeki shortened his steps.

Together they turned right into the broad street, passing the front of the Wayfarer Temple. A couple of familiar cloaked figures waved to the priests and descended the wider circular stairs leading to the street. Two watchers with bored faces stood to one side.

'Baba!' Zadeki called out.

His father turned and gripped Aunt Bikan's shoulder. Both changed direction to come their way. 'You're heading home early.'

'We thought we should check on Delvina.'

They continued down the unusually empty street. A light breeze ruffled the drooping trees and sent water spilling onto the pavement from a nearby fountain. In the distance, the thunder grew louder.

Boom, boom, ba-boom.

A bell rang out, vibrating deep and loud, followed by the sound of many feet running down the Council stairs from behind.

'Get to the side,' Baba yelled, he took Gentle Ariel by the arm.

Zadeki grabbed Danel and dragged him out of the way a moment or two before a group of watchers, four abreast and twenty deep, marched past with truncheons and whips at the ready.

'The rioters must have broken through the barricade,' Ariel panted, her eyes big as two dark wells.

'We need to get back to the house and see if Delvina and the others are alright,' Zadeki urged.

'Let's go the back route,' Aunt Bikan said, heading toward the laneway.

Even as she spoke, eight watchers peeled off the main group and headed their way. Zadeki blinked. The bumptious Lord Hale was in the lead.

'You, Flame-get there, the Grand Technician would speak with you. Now!'

'At last,' Zadeki murmured.

Their research had made it clear that the Grand Technician would know how a soul-bond seal's ownership was transferred. Perhaps, now he was ready to tell them what he knew. Though why assign so many watchers for a simple request? The itching beneath his shoulder ramped up.

Aunt Bikan held up her hands, palms out. 'Of course, Lord Hale, but first we wish to check on our friend.'

'This is not a request. Technician Iulien wants to see you without a moment's delay.'

Aunt Bikan's angular frame stiffened, no doubt irritated by the Vaane lord's commanding tone.' Her lean chest rose and fell and she inclined her head. 'Of course. I will come while the others check ...'

'You three flame-get. The Grand Technician was quite explicit.'

Zadeki's muscles tightened. There was no mistaking the veiled threat. Baba and Bikan exchanged a look. Could they refuse such a clear order? The watchers circled in tighter, menace in their movements.

'Perhaps it might be best to see what he wants,' Baba said.

Aunt Bikan grimaced. She turned back to Lord Hale. 'We will come as requested. Can you give us a moment to speak to our companions?'

'Make it fast.'

'Danel, go with Ariel and see that Delvina is safe.'

'But what about you? Shouldn't I come with you?'

'I don't think that would be wise.'

'Then, should you go?'

'We will be fine.' And then in a lower voice, pitched so the watchers couldn't hear. 'If we have to fight our way out, we will. Remember, whatever happens Danel, you must get the information we've gleaned back to Havilah.' With subtle movements, she slipped a piece of paper in Danel's hand. 'If we don't return by nightfall, go with Samwin and Ariel to Destruction Bay and find the Mariner Habbiah.'

Zadeki frowned. 'We could take them now, beneath open skies.'

'We'll find out what Iulien, the son of Gaian wants, first.'

Baba nudged Zadeki. 'It will give time for our friends to get some distance from here and for Danel to find Delvina.'

Zadeki nodded. Their first thought had to be for the Darane under their protection. It might be better to resist without the restriction of ceilings, but not if their opponents could take more vulnerable hostages.

More watchers streamed down the stairs. How many were there?

Aunt Bikan brushed Zadeki's shoulder. 'If you get the chance to slip away, go at once and help your friends.'

'That's enough. 'Lord Hale stepped closer, his sword raised.

Baba held up both his hands. 'Peace. We're coming.'

Aunt Bikan and Baba followed the watchers, and Zadeki reluctantly fell in step. Six watchers closed in behind them.

Zadeki's gut twisted. This was not a friendly escort. The watchers' faces were grim, their eyes nervous. Zadeki rubbed his hands on the ridiculous Vaane cloak, taking care not to trip on it as they marched up the stairs to the Council Chambers.

Going into the building, walking down the hall,

entering the Council Chamber seemed a terrible idea, fraught with danger.

But Bikan was right. If Danel and Delvina could slip away, he and the others would be freer to shapeshift and join them at the cove if the Vaane turned against them.

Retza pulled on his boots and straightened his watcher-jacket. His knee throbbed, but he could put some weight on it now that Barekia had strapped it. The old Scrybe insisted he needed to rest a bit longer, but after four days of lying around, he had to do something.

He limped to the door and pushed it open. Hand on the wall, he hobbled as fast as he could toward the access door at the end of the tunnel. The watcher quarters were on the other side of the Grand Cavern, not so far on a good day. A long line of glimmer lights stretched down the corridor. Voices echoed from Havilah's ready room further down the passage. It sounded like a meeting, one he hadn't been invited to. Nor could he think of any reason he could gate crash. He wasn't on duty yet, had no messages or news to report. Perhaps Secondwun Timon could update him on the important stuff.

He saluted the two watchers standing outside the door and shuffled past them. A trio of tall Forest Folk swung into view at the end of the corridor. At the same time, the door to the ready room opened and Gilarth stepped out.

'Retza! I thought you were still recovering!' The big watcher's startled gaze slid from Retza to the group striding toward them.

Gilarth gripped Retza's shoulder with rock-like fingers. 'You stay put,' he said before turning to greet the newcomers. 'Kinleader.'

Retza nodded and peered past Gilarth's bulk.

The Kinleader, Telsima, walked in front of two taller Forest Folk, Zadeki's older brother, Josenif, and one of the koraktil-shifters, an older man.

'Son of the mountain.' Telsima inclined her head to Gilarth, the gimmer lights giving the white streaks in her hair a bluish tinge. 'Zadeki's friend.' She beamed a smile at Retza. 'Is Elad's daughter available?'

'Should be,' Gilarth said. 'We've been hoping you would return.' He stood aside to allow the Forest Folk to enter the room, then steered Retza inside.

Overseer Havilah sat next to a bony toolwun. With a shock, Retza realised it was Karel, Secondwun of the Greenstone South. She was rake-thin, her eyes huge in their shadowed sockets. Both her hands were curled around a steaming mug.

Havilah stood and smoothed down her skirt. 'Kinleader. We're so glad you're here. Come into my office.' Once they'd all filed in, the Overseer turned to the Forest Folk. 'Do you have news?'

'Yes, some good news, I hope,' Telsima responded. 'While the flooding damaged the sava harvest, the receding waters have triggered an abundance of fish. We have caught extra and dried and smoked them for preservation. It should help your situation for a day or two at least.'

'Every bit helps. Our stores grow lower each day, and while our potato harvest looks promising, the earliest we can harvest is still many rosters away. Any news from Tarka?'

'The maize harvest goes well. Supak Kapok will send the agreed amount by yarma train in a day or two. Serafin, here, and Perdak will fly as much of the harvest as they can carry before it leaves on yarma-back.'

'I'm glad to hear it.' Some of the tension eased from Havilah's face.

Retza let out a breath and leaned part of his weight against the wall. Extra rations would be welcome. Enough hopefully to keep them going until the yarma train arrived in just over a ten-day. But only if they could open the Gate.

'We also have good news and bad.' Havilah said. 'We found and rescued the survivors of Greenstone South crew, in large part, due to Watcher Retza's efforts.' Overseer Havilah threw him a rare smile then scowled. 'Who I thought was recovering.'

Retza flushed as all eyes turned in his direction. He lifted his chin and ignored the tremble in his aching leg. 'I'm ready for light duties at least, ma'am.'

Havilah snorted and Josenif gave him a crooked grin.

Telsima touched his shoulder. 'Even so, perhaps you should sit, son of rock.'

Gilarth pushed him onto a stool. 'And maybe Barekia and I should be the judges of that, Watcher.'

'And what is the bad news, daughter of Elad?' Telsima asked. 'How many lives were lost?'

A look of wonder flashed through Havilah's amethyst eyes. 'None, though Lead Hand of Greenstone South and a few of the others are in a bad way. Scrybe Barekia has turned the Heart Room into a makeshift clinic and is doing what she can for them.

Kinleader Telsima nodded. 'I will stop by later and see if I can help. But this is not what is disturbing you.'

'We're royally jiggered,' Nebam barked.

Retza jumped, only now noticing Havilah's Secondwun slouched in the corner of the room, his head bandaged and his right arm in a sling.

Nebam made a face, then spread out his left hand. 'The tunnel is flooded and opens onto a massive underground lake. We've been unable to determine its extent or even its depth. In the time we have, there is no way through, under or around it. We won't be able to pump the water elsewhere, so we can't continue our tunnelling operations, even if the area was stable enough.'

'Have we heard from Highwun Bikan?' Retza asked. Perhaps Del and Zadeki were on their way home already with vital clues to finding the old Overseer or the seal. If they could open the Gate, they wouldn't need the tunnel.

Telsima and Josenif exchanged glances. Retza's heart beat harder. Had something happened to the delegation?

Josenif ran his hand through his dark curls, so like Zadeki's. 'I spoke with the Tamrin watermen that took the party to Redhaven. Da-Sestru left a message with them. The Warden was unable to help and has been out of communication with the Lonely Isles at least three of the silver moon's cycles. The Warden sent his last remaining ship to find out what happened and Elder Bikan and the others went with them to seek the answers to the Seal from the Sea Dragon Throne.'

'When did they leave?' Retza's throat seized. His twin was even further away, heading into more danger and now separated from him by an ocean.

'Over a ten-day ago. They could be on their way back by now, if they met with success. Or it might take longer to ... negotiate ... with the Vaane.'

'And have you found a viable way from the King's Road to the Cauldron as a backup plan?'

'A possible route, though it's dangerous and will double the time of the journey.'

'Too late to be much use.' Havilah put her hands

behind her back, her face bleak. 'Let's pray they find the answers we need. Unless we can open the Gate in a ten-day, we will starve.'

'If we can, we will prevent that happening, earth sister. And, if you like, Josenif can help with your search for the Overseer's seal.'

'That would be appreciated, Kinleader.'

'Good. If you don't mind, we will rest now and speak with you later.'

As soon as the door closed behind the Forest Folk, Nebam banged the conference table with his fist. 'We are searching in the wrong places. Uzza's brat knows more than she's telling, I'd wager an eye on it.'

'Nebam!' Havilah frowned. 'Has Zara said anything at all, Gilarth?'

'No.' Gilarth folded his arms across his broad chest. 'I won't be party to any harm coming to Zara and Jesson, Overseer.'

'Even if it means we all starve.'

Gilarth's expression solidified like cooling slag. 'I believe gentle persuasion would be more effective. Retza has influence with the Lady Zara.'

'I don't want to use harsher methods, unless I have to.' Overseer Havilah held Gilarth's gaze a long moment, then glanced at Retza. 'So, Watcher, did you glean any information from Zara on your earlier shifts?'

Retza swallowed hard. 'No, ma'am. She refused to talk and then the cave-in happened ....'

Havilah drummed her fingers on the table. 'Watcher Retza, I will approve your return to active duty. You are assigned to Zara until further notice. Explain the situation to her, ask her if she knows anything about the seal or the possible whereabouts of her father.'

'Begging your pardon, couldn't you or Gilarth ask her? I'm no different to her than any other lowwun.'

Havilah sat back in her chair. 'She considers Gilarth a traitor for siding with us, and me as the usurper of her father's position. She seems to have some connection with you and Delvina.'

Gilarth rumbled a laugh. 'She's been asking about you every day since the cave-in. You're our best bet.'

'We need answers, Retza, and soon. Gilarth was right to enlist you.'

'Yes, ma'am. I will do my best.'

The praise warmed him, but somehow he still felt hollow. If Delvina was here, she'd know how to approach the prickly highwun, but he'd rather wade through a thousand lek of murky floodwater than try to sweet talk Lady Zara. Gilarth had to be crazy to think she cared for anyone but her brother and family. Hopefully Delvina and Zadeki would return soon with all they needed to know about the seal and save him from his latest crazy assignment.

'That will be all, Watcher. Thank you for your help. Our lives may depend on your success.'

No petitioners crowded at the throne room today. Instead, watchers stood at the doors and around the walls, truncheons drawn. The Grand Technician paced in front of the empty throne. Zadeki's chest squeezed tight and any illusion of a friendly meeting frayed into nothingness. He only wished the confrontation could be under an open sky.

Lord Hale halted in front of the Grand Technician. 'Here they are, Iulien.'

'Just three? Where are the two ebed?' The Grand Technician spluttered, his face pinking.

'Ebed? I did not see them, just Gentle Ariel and her retainer.'

The Grand Technician made an impatient gesture. 'Never mind. We can find them later.'

Aunt Bikan stepped past Lord Hale, her dark eyes snapping. 'What is this about Iulien, son of Gaian.'

'You know full well. Did you think your treachery would go unnoticed?'

'We have kept to the terms of the agreement. No shapeshifting ...'

'That is not so!' The Grand Technician pointed a shaking finger at them. 'You have been consorting with the crystal singers, frequenting the crafters' quarters, ransacking the libraries.'

'To discover solutions to the children of Darian's problem. None of these things were forbidden.'

'You quibble. Your base aims are transparent. You mean to provoke rebellion against our rightful liege, Prince Selwin.'

'He is not our King, nor do we have any desire to live upon this island. The little prince is welcome to his grandfather's throne.'

'You can no longer fool us. How long have you been on the Island? When did you start plotting against us? Did you previously sneak aboard compatriots to prepare for your coming? Now the rabble march toward Silantis. But you already know this.'

Baba pulled back his heavy hood. 'We arrived but days ago. We have nothing to do with this rebellion.'

'Then can you explain this?' The Grand Technician held up an eagle's feather. 'This, Gentle Bikan,' his voice laden with scorn, 'was found on the person of one of the conspirators. The bird it comes from is only found on the mainland.'

Zadeki stared at the feather. The Grand Technician's claims were laughable. His Kin had nothing to do with the ebed rebellion, he was sure of it. But why would one of the rebel ebeds carry such a thing and what had his elders been doing, the days he and the other two searched the library?

'I know not how the feather came here, but if this is the flimsy evidence you base your accusations on, it's laughable,' Aunt Bikan said.

The Grand Technician made a hand signal. A watcher brought forward a slight figure. Irina. Zadeki's eyes flew open. Was the ebed woman here willingly or under duress?

'This loyal ebed overheard you encouraging rebellion. Your plan to overturn the rightful heir and reinstate your monstrous rule has been exposed. Admit it, submit to justice and we will show you mercy.'

'So much for the hospitality of the children of starshine.' Aunt Bikan's mouth twisted. 'Whatever the girl overhead, it was not plans of treason or invasion. Surely you have stronger evidence than this? No? Because there is none.'

'This is your trial and you have been found guilty of highest treason.' The Grand Technician waved his hand, and three watchers carrying chains of a dark, shimmering metal, stepped forward.

Aunt Bikan laughed. 'You think you can capture us?'

Baba nudged Zadeki and pointed his chin toward the balcony that surrounded the chamber. 'Watchers up there,' he breathed. 'Wait for Da-Sestru's signal.'

Lord Hale smirked. 'These bonds have been infused with shadow crystals.'

Aunt Bikan's face tightened. 'Then it is true—'

'Restrain them,' Lord Hale shouted. 'Take them alive if you can, dead if you have to.'

The watchers fanned out and advanced warily.

'You have to catch us first.' Bikan discarded the thick, woollen cloak like an outgrown cocoon, entangling the closest watcher with it, then twirled and kicked another in the midriff. The man staggered back. His companions rushed forward. She leapt into the air, taking on her crested eagle form.

Zadeki dropped his cloak, barrelling a watcher out of the way, and leapt after her. He felt the familiar transformation ripple through his limbs and torso, his arms changing to wings, his bones hollowing, his organs transforming, his legs shrinking. With a powerful downstroke, he rose in the air though with less momentum without the normal run-up.

Baba rose beside him. They spiralled upward toward the skylight.

The Grand Technician scurried backward. 'Fools, you can't get out.'

'I'll break the glass,' Baba keened.

A twang and a soft hiss. An arrow sliced through the air, ruffling Zadeki's tail feathers. His heart hammered against his ribs. Archers on the balcony. Of course. He pumped his wings harder and rocked from side to side to present less of a target.

'I'll distract them. Zadeki find your friends and get them to safety,' Aunt Bikan keened on the other side.

She dived toward the balcony with a flurry of wings and feathers. A long whistling cry tore through the tumult. Archers ducked and dodged the raking of her hooked beak and sharp claws.

Crack. A shower of painted glass cascaded to the floor. 'Zadeki, fly higher,' Baba called.

More watchers streamed onto the balcony. Aunt Bikan would soon be outnumbered. He dove down, sharp beak aimed at her attacker.

'Youngest son. Come. Don't turn back.'

Zadeki dodged a truncheon thrown at him, swooped and raked his beak across a watcher's face. The watcher turned from his attack on Bikan and swiped at him with a long knife. Zadeki caught the weapon with his claws, wrenching it from the man's grasp. It clattered to the floor far below and the watcher lost her balance and followed.

He filtered out the wail of despair, the sickening thump.

'Come on, Aunt,' he screeched. 'I've got you covered.'

'Watch out,' Baba cried.

An arrow spiralled towards him. He pushed down on his wings, to dodge the missile, but his legs were caught in someone's cloak. He pulled, and dipped and twisted down, breaking free of the entanglement, but it would already be too late.

A flurry of feathers and Aunt Bikan was in front of him.

'No, Da-Sestru.'

He felt the thud rather than heard it. She hovered a moment in the air, then, with a squawk, fell tumbling to the floor below.

Baba was beside him.

'We have to help her,' Zadeki keened.

'I will. Go, find your friends.'

He pushed Zadeki toward the roof, but they had both lost height. More watchers stepped out onto the balcony. They threw a dark shape at them and it spread out like a flock of birds pivoting in the sky.

A weight fell on him, enmeshing his wings and legs and beak, pulling him downward. Darkness clouded his vision, weakened his hold on the eagle form.

He couldn't fly.

He dropped out of the air, hitting the ground hard.

The heavy clump of watcher boots echoed in the corridor outside. Another change of shift. Another scanty meal. Another endless day of waiting for an uncertain fate. Zara pressed her flaking lips together and watched at the nod of Jesson's bright hair as he lay belly first on the floor pushing around his makeshift diggers and glimmer trucks.

The door swung open, letting in a brief gust of air and the musty smell of wet stone, before closing with a solid clunk. For once Jesson didn't stir. Perhaps for him, as for her, the dreaded hunger pains had deadened, and the thought of more softened algae induced the urge to puke. She stared at her chipped and flaking fingernails.

'Your meal, Lady Zara,' a familiar gruff voice said.

Zara's chest fluttered, and she gripped the table's sharp edge. It wasn't him. It couldn't be. He was trapped beneath tons of rock, or so they said.

The watcher stepped closer. She could hear him take a breath, feel his nearness, detect a faint dry scent of rock dust, algae and sweat.

'What are you writing, my Lady?'

She stared down at the blank page and the dried inky

tip of the stylus in front of her. She hadn't written anything for days. 'What business is that of yours, Watcher?' she snapped.

His low chuckle had a wry twist. 'Not changed I see. Good old Zara. Always the soft reply.'

She whipped around and glared into Retza's clear grey eyes. His face was thinner and marred with scratches and scrapes, but he stood as solid and sturdy as ever, handsome in bat-leather.

Jesson twisted around, a huge grin spreading across his thin face. 'Retza! Where have you been?' He jumped up and hugged the watcher's knees. 'You haven't come for ages,' he accused.

'You're supposed to be dead,' Zara added, unable to keep the reproach out of her voice. 'Gilarth said you'd been caught in a cave-in.'

'Sorry to disappoint, my Lady.'

'Zara! You didn't tell me.' Jesson twisted around to glare at her.

'I ... I didn't want to upset you, Jessi.' She bent her head, allowing her hair to hide her burning cheeks. Her heart thumped painfully. She couldn't, wouldn't let Retza see she cared. It was a weakness she couldn't afford. He was the enemy.

A shuffling sound and Retza placed the tray of food on a cleared spot on the table, Jesson still clinging to his leg. A delicious smell tickled her nostrils and her mouth watered. Fish? Surely not. Her hands shaking, she lifted the cover to display two small dried fish cooked in mushrooms and algae. On the side, six plump red berries. Which showed how severe their plight was, that such a meagre meal seemed a feast.

Jesson jumped up, his eyes as big as his face. 'Is that for us?'

Retza ruffled Jesson's white-gold hair. 'Enjoy it while it lasts, scamp. The Forest Folk arrived with some food to give a little bit of variety to our usual fare.'

He leaned forward, placed a small box on the edge of the table and pushed it toward her. His fingers were strong and calloused but clean, with no grime caked under the blunt nails. Nestled in the box was a small cake of scented soap and a bag of marbles; something for her, something for Jesson, an unexpected kindness. Her throat tightened on a roster-full of unshed tears.

Retza's shadow moved from the table as he took his position. She gave him a sideways look. He was dashing in watcher black, stronger and more confident than the first time she'd seen him, his face more sculpted, his manner more confident.

She could almost believe he cared. Almost. But more likely he wanted information from her.

Jesson picked up his fish with his fingers and scoffed it down. She didn't scold. What was the point anymore? But she did do her best to eat more daintily. Not an easy task, with the reawakened hunger pangs clawing at her stomach.

She patted her mouth with the cloth provided and studied Retza's impassive face. 'Are we ... are the food stores still short?' she whispered.

Retza hooked his thumbs in his belt, hesitated then nodded as though making up his mind. 'We're short, it's true. The potato farms took blight when the Crystal Heart was out, but Leadwun Gregan has replanted the farms and Delvina and Danel are searching for more supplies from outside.'

'Yes, I know that. Gilarth told me.' That didn't explain the nail-biting tension in the air, in the stance and voices and eyes of the watchers or Barekia's harried frown ever since the first groundquake. 'The second collapse didn't seem as bad as the first.'

Strong emotions filtered across Retza's blunt face. He lowered his voice. 'I was trapped down there for a while. It wasn't good.'

'How is your sister, Delvina? Has she returned from her journey?'

Retza turned his head away, then sighed. 'She went with the delegation. They've gone on to the Lonely Isles and we haven't heard from them since.'

'That's a long way to go. She is brave.'

'She is.' Retza nodded. 'I was angry that she went. She'd agreed to join the watchers with me, but then changed her mind without telling me.'

'Perhaps, she needs to chart her own course.'

'Maybe. At least she need not starve with us.'

Zara could see the worry on his face. Was it really that desperate? 'But the Tamrin are bringing food.'

'Yes, but with the Gate shut and the tunnel no longer viable, it's getting the supplies into the mountain that's the problem. If we have to haul them up to the Cauldron—with cliffs, and glaciers and snowstorms to battle, it's likely they'll arrive too late to do much good.'

'But you can start again. Redo the tunnel.'

'No, Zara, we can't. The flooding is too severe.' He closed his eyes a moment, took a deep breath. Something in his face hardened. 'We need to open the Gate. We need the seal or some way to bypass it. It's the only way now.'

'If you hadn't deposed my father, you wouldn't be in this mess.'

'No, my sister would be dead. And likely all of us when your father's sacrifice proved useless at restarting the Crystal Heart.' He placed his hands on the table. 'Zara this isn't a game. The lives of everyone in the realm is at stake.'

'Baba—'

'His too, if he still lives, and yours and Jesson's.' He turned away abruptly, and his hand tightened on the truncheon.

Jesson whimpered. 'You won't let us die, will you Retza? Baba's coming back.'

Retza spun around again 'No, he's not.' Retza closed his eyes, took a deep breath. 'Look, sorry, I know he's your baba. We're working on opening the Gate in time so that you don't starve along with the rest of us. Do you know where your father or the seal might be or how we can open the Gate ...?"

How was she supposed to know? And even if she did, wouldn't she be betraying Baba and her family if she told them? But Retza was right. She and Jesson would starve along with the others. And Baba? Why hadn't he come back yet to reclaim the realm? Was he in some dire trouble? Perhaps he did need to be rescued. The more she learned, the more she doubted that Baba had always chosen right. 'Will you let Jesson and me go, and not harm Baba and the others if you find them?'

Retza's eyes clouded. 'I'm not sure Havilah could agree to that, but I can do the best I can.'

She glared at him.

'Zara, you may think we are below you, that our lives don't matter, that only highwuns like your baba are important. Delvina and I, we've been on our own since our parents died in the cave-in and then our da-baba died too.'

Zara turned her head away, wondering where he was

going with this. Her throat tightened. Was what he said true?

'There are four thousand people, toolwuns, oldwuns, littlewuns. All slowly starving—'

'Over five thousand,' she said, catching him with an inaccuracy.

'Once. People are dying. We need to disarm the Gate and only your baba or his seal can do that. Maybe Havilah would do a deal to save all those lives. What about you?'

She bowed her head. How could she be disloyal to Baba? How could she not with so many lives at stake? Including hers and Jesson's.

'Zara, Baba wouldn't want all those people to die, would he?'

She wanted to ignore the plea and fright in Jesson's eyes. But she couldn't. Baba might already be dead. But she could save Jesson. And Retza, an inner voice whispered.

She twisted her skirt between shaking fingers. Tears gathered in the corners of her eyes. 'I ... I don't know much. But I did overhear Baba tell my brother Asrab ...' her voice choked.

Retza brushed her shoulder. 'Yes?'

She cleared her throat. 'Um ... he said that in extreme danger, to meet at Temple's Rest.'

'Temple's Rest? And where is that? Gilarth searched the Sunken Temple.'

'That's all I know.'

'Well, it's something. Thank you, Zara.'

Zara lifted her head, her cheeks warming. She was right to tell him. At least, she hoped so.

The weighted net settled over Zadeki, made of the same dark materials as the shackles. Shadowy energy burrowed into him. It clawed at his powers, shredded his focus, threatened his sense of being. If he shifted now, he could get lost in the transition.

Baba lay beside him in human form, stunned by the fall and caught in the net.

Beyond him, an eagle lay crumpled in the centre of the Crystal Star. Aunt Bikan's eagle form shimmered and changed. The arrow remained, piercing her breast and doing irreparable damage to transitioning tissues. Scarlet and crimson blood seeped out and soaked Aunt Bikan's white tari in a red bloom.

'She needs help,' Zadeki raged, keeping a tenuous grip on his eagle shape.

'She got what she deserved,' the Grand Technician responded. 'Come quietly, and you will not be harmed.'

A dozen archers clattered down the stairs and surrounded them, arrows pointing at them. Baba shook his head and struggled to fly toward Aunt Bikan, but the net pulled him back to the floor with every move.

'Father's sister,' Baba keened.

Her eyes fluttered open. 'Peace. I'm going home.'

Was she delirious? 'You said it would be alright,' Zadeki growled.

Bikan turned her head and looked at him, a sudden clarity in her bright eyes. 'It will be. You will see, impatient one.' Blood trickled from the corner of her mouth, a crimson snake against the white shimmer of her skin. 'Don't despair.' Her voice faded, and with one last sigh, her life force slipped away.

Tears ran down Baba's face. 'Be at peace, daughter of the forest.' He whispered.

Zadeki shuddered. How could this be? She tried to save them. Now she was dead, and they were caught fast, like fat flies in a spiderweb. Had it all been for nothing?

He dredged up every last fragment of power, every shred of rage, and forced the dangerous shift eagle to jaguar form, ready to tear and bite and maim. It felt like wading through debris-choked floodwaters, but he did it. His tail lashed against the dark weave and he turned toward the Grand Technician just a pace or two away.

Despite the way the net frayed at his focus and entangled his limbs, he was sure he could take the traitor down before the arrows pierced him.

Baba lunged toward him, pulled him back. 'Wait.'

'They mean to kill us anyway.'

'Not quite yet,' a cool alto purred. Princess Avardin appeared from one of the archways, her robes catching the outside light like sunshine on water. 'Thank you, Iulien.'

'What?' The Grand Technician turned and stared at her, his face slack with shock. He pulled himself together. 'Princess Avardin, this is no concern of yours.'

'Fool, of course it is. You can never see what is happening under your long nose, never act without dithering, always too late and too slow. Which is why I am relieving you of authority as regent.'

A group of armed ebed crowded in behind her. Angry men, with ripped clothes and ash-stained faces.

The Grand Technician drew himself up to his considerable height. His eyes narrowed. 'You have no right! Are you colluding with these monstrous shapeshifters?'

Zadeki held still. Had Delvina spoken to the Princess and persuaded her to take their side? If only she had intervened moments earlier before Aunt Bikan was struck down. Rage curled in his muscles. Zadeki turned first one way, then the other, not sure who he should attack or whether he could break free of the net.

Princess Avardin smiled with the friendliness of a python. 'I have every right. You have overstepped your station, puffed yourself up with importance, usurped the Sea Dragon King's throne.'

'It was your uncle's stated wish that I be Regent and protector of his grandson. I bear the seal of authority. Watchers, arrest her.'

No one moved.

'Watchers, why do you hesitate? I am your lawful Regent. Do as I say? Lord Hale, have you nothing to say to this treachery?'

Lord Hale moved to stand with the Princess. 'Iulien, you are a weak excuse for a regent. Always have been.'

Zadeki shivered. Hale was no friend of theirs. He had argued loudest against them. If he supported Avardin, as he seemed to do, then this was no rescue. He glanced at Baba and he could see the same truth in his eyes. Zadeki bunched his muscles, and while the Vaane high ones were distracted, wiggled against the weight and constraints of the net, creeping toward its edge tinas by tinas. Baba nodded in approval and did the same.

'But, but, I've acted as you wished. I have taken the shapeshifters prisoner. Would have done so sooner if the Princess hadn't spoken on their behalf.' The Grand Technician's gaze darted from Avardin to Hale, horror dawning in his eyes. 'You set me up. The Council will not accept this travesty. I will—'

The twang of a bowstring, the hiss as an arrow flying straight, followed by a dull thud and a grunt. The Grand Technician crumpled to the floor, clutching at the long shaft in his chest. Fitting, given this was how Aunt Bikan had died.

Avardin lowered her bow. 'Unpleasant, but necessary.' She walked around the netting, her long skirts swishing against the stone tiles, to kneel beside the twitching Grand Technician.

'Fool. I will never transfer the Regent's soul-bond to you,' he snarled.

'Not to worry. I'll work it out.' She lifted the crystal pendant from beneath the Grand Technician's brocaded robes and pulled. The fine gold chain snapped. 'This is all I need.'

'What should we do with these two Flame-get?' Lord Hale asked.

Avardin turned back, her opalescent eyes sweeping over them. 'Kill them ...' The creak of bowstrings sent a shiver up Zadeki's spine. Restrained beneath the nets, they were easy targets. 'No wait, they may have information useful for my future plans. Chain them and secure them in the Hole.'

'Are you sure, Avardin? They're dangerous creatures and hard to restrain.'

Zadeki crept closer, fighting against the bleed of energy.

'Indeed, but I'm more dangerous.' She spun, her eyes snaring his. 'By the way, little cub, you may like to know that I have Delvina. She told me everything. She sees you for the monster you are.'

Something twisted inside Zadeki. It wasn't true. It couldn't be. Delvina wouldn't betray them. A roar triggered like an avalanche and rumbled through his chest. He leapt for the tormenting woman. The net jerked him back and fire seared through him. Then darkness.

Delvina blinked and rubbed her eyes, her head full of spider silk and the dregs of dark dreams. The room was wrapped in shadows. Where was she? Her last memory was of sitting in the aviary ... no, of Princess Avardin's cool hand on her elbow, guiding her to the main house to wait for the carriage. Delvina moistened her dry mouth and sat up in a rumpled bed. A decorated screen divided the space. Hot-white light seeped through the gaps in the shuttered windows, throwing bars across the tiled floor. The aroma of wax and dead flowers perfumed the room.

How had she slept so long and deep? She must have been more tired than she'd realised. She'd better get back to the Mariner's House before her friends returned and realised she was missing.

She stood and swayed, catching onto the carved bedhead. After a moment, she staggered to the door, still woozy. She jiggled the latch, pulled and pushed but the door wouldn't budge. Locked. She hammered on the wood panelling. 'Hey, let me out!'

After some moments, footsteps hurried towards her, followed by the sound of a lock turning and a click. The door swung open. The maid from the aviary, Maia, stood peering into the room. Delvina covered her eyes at the sudden light.

'I must go back to my friends.'

'Princess Avardin wishes to speak to you before you leave.'

'I'm ...' Would it be rude to refuse. She wouldn't take long. 'Well, I guess.'

She went to step over the threshold, but the servant didn't move out of the way.

'You cannot appear before the Princess with rumpled clothes and the dirt of the day. I will take you to the bathing area.'

More delays. Delvina opened her mouth to insist, but suddenly became aware of the pressure of her bladder and a taste in her mouth like day-old snails. 'If it's quick.'

Maia led her along a corridor and down some stairs to a large tiled room with a scented pool full of steaming water. The maid reached up to unfasten Delvina's brocaded jacket with the Mariner's colours and sea dragon pattern.

'Hey, what are you doing?' Delvina batted the girl's hands away.

'Assisting you bathe, Gentle.'

'Well, I can do that by myself.'

Maia hesitated, then bowed. 'As you wish. The water closet is over there. Please, don't take too long.'

When Delvina finished the necessary, she slipped into the pool. She closed her eyes and allowed the warm sweet-smelling water to ease her muscles and worries. Just for a moment. This was so different from the quick, lukewarm showers in the cribrooms at home or even the bathing room in the Mariner's house. As tempting as it was, she shouldn't tarry. When she opened her eyes, she noticed a warm fluffy towel with a pile of fresh new clothes with Lady Avardin's insignia on it. Her old clothes had disappeared.

She dried herself and dressed as quickly as she could. The door swung open and Maia walked in. 'Please, come quick. The Mistress is asking for you.'

'Where are my boots?'

'They were soiled. Follow me.'

Maia set off at a fast clip, and Delvina hurried after her barefooted.

At least it was still light. If anything, the day seemed to have grown brighter. Perhaps there had been a thunderstorm while she slept. She remembered the low, continuous rumble before she fell asleep. And she had to admit, she did feel refreshed and comfortable in the clean, sweet smelling clothes, softer and more richly adorned than those she had been wearing. Did it matter whose livery she wore?

Maia led her through many twists and turns, along corridors, past rooms, down stairs and across landings. Despite growing up in a maze of underground tunnels, Delvina had a hard time keeping her sense of direction. At last they approached finely-carved and gilded doors and stepped into an airy room, with the central part of the ceiling open to a patch of sky. A long pool where golden fish darted among lily pads ran down the centre of the room. Lacy plants in pots, graceful statues and embroidered partitions adorned airy spaces, giving it a luxurious feel.

Princess Avardin stepped out from an alcove, a satisfied look on her sculpted face. Her blue-black hair cascaded down her back and a bright plumed bird perched on her silvery-white fingers. 'Ah, so our little guest is awake. Please join me for a meal.'

Delvina stood her ground. 'It's a generous offer, Your Honour, but I should get back to my friends.'

A shadow fell over the beautiful face. 'Of course, you slept through it. You would not know.'

What could have happened? How long had she slept? A cold hand seemed to tug at her heart. 'My Lady?'

'Please, sit down.' Avardin lifted her hand and the jewel-like bird took flight and settled on top of a screen. The princess strolled towards a nook housing a table and two chairs. Delicious smells beckoned, and Delvina realised she was ravenous.

She hurried over and sat in the chair the Lady indicated. Platters were heaped with food—the crusty rolls, jars of honey, fish fried with dill, rounds of cheese. The image of Retza's gaunt and hungry face pulled at her conscience. Yet not eating wouldn't help him. She tucked in.

Once the edge of her hunger was dulled, Delvina looked up to find the Princess gazing at her with an amused smile. Delvina wiped her hands on a napkin and flushed. 'Forgive me if I ate in haste.'

Avardin took a delicate bite of a rich, red fruit and then touched a cloth to her lips. 'Not at all.' She continued to stare. 'Your colouring is unusual for an ebed. Paler even than Maia. Is it natural?' Her fingers brushed Delvina's hand.

'Yes.' Delvina squirmed, suddenly feeling uneasy. What was this woman's interest in her?

'I'm a collector. I like collecting unusual things.' The words eerily seemed to answer Delvina's thoughts. 'I've brought over a thousand countless oddities from the land across the ocean. I think you and your friend, Danel, look … quaint with your pale, freckled skin, light eyes and hair, as though the colour has been bleached out of you. It's such a pity.'

The woman's final words pinged in Delvina's thoughts. 'What's a pity?'

'You slept through a wild and chaotic night.'

'Night?'

'Yes.' Avardin smiled.

Delvina stood up, sending a dish smashing to the tiled floor. 'I must get back ...'

'Oh no, my little bird. The rebels broke through the barrier yesterday and marched on Silantis, destroying homes and setting them on fire.'

Cold dread settled in her stomach, curdling the food she'd just eaten. 'The Mariner's House?'

'Burnt to the ground.'

'My friends, did they get away. Danel? Zadeki? The others?'

Avardin's gaze did not waver. 'Sad to say, I don't know what happened to Danel or the Mariner's daughter. Until we sift through the ashes ...'

Delvina dropped back into the chair like a stone. 'No, but ...' Why hadn't he Forest Folk saved them? Zadeki would've been with them.

'As for these Forest Folk. They were not in the house at the time. No, it grieves me to say they are not the friends you thought them to be.'

Delvina shook her head. The walls closing in. What the woman was saying couldn't be true. 'Zadeki—.'

'The youngling was with his elders.' Avardin smoothed the cloth draping the table. 'Perhaps innocent to their plots and schemes.'

'What do you mean?'

'It appears the Forest Folk, as you call them, were aiding and abetting the rebels. They helped them invade the Council Chambers. Before we could defeat them, the Grand Technician, Iulien, was killed.'

It didn't make any sense. Why would they ... and how? Delvina frowned. What were Korak and Bikan doing during the days she and the others were in the library?

'They were helping us.'

'That was their pretext, yes. But my dear, they used you to get access to the island. Something they have been denied ever since they were evicted as the troublemakers they are. It has ever been their desire to depose the rightful rule of the Sea Dragon King and they nearly succeeded, if my watchers hadn't acted so quickly to contain them. Even now, my sweet cousin might be dead along with his former Regent.' Avardin smiled. 'And I have you to thank for this. Your confidences yesterday were invaluable. So, in return, I offer you sanctuary in my household.'

'I ... no, I must go back to the Glittering Realms, to let Havilah know what happened.'

'Yes, in time perhaps. You must understand, as a companion of the traitors, your life is forfeit, but I have pointed out to the Council that you were caught up as an innocent in their cunning.'

Delvina pushed herself up, her legs like water. 'I should go search ...'

'Don't torment yourself. Your companions are dead, and in a fire so hot, there would not be much left but ashes. You should be careful who you trust, my sweet.'

Delvina groaned. This could not be happening. Danel and Ariel dead. Zadeki and the others, traitors. No, she couldn't, wouldn't believe it.

Princess Avardin's strange eyes seemed to snare her and the pressure to sit grew too hard to resist.

She sighed and sank back down. 'Then all is lost.'

'Perhaps not,' Avardin'sen voice was soft as fingertips brushing over a lover's skin. 'I will be your advocate before the Council. In fact, I imagine I will soon be appointed as the new Regent. If we can broker a deal for the crystals you supply, I will do everything I can to help you open the gate to your realm. 'I assure you, my little bird, I am your true friend. We will soon set things right.'

It was blacker even than in the Darane's deep caverns and tunnels. He hung in the void, like a rotten fruit on a bare branch, though for all he knew, he might be upside down.

No glimmer torches or glow-worms to lighten the dark. No breath of air in the turbid stillness. No sound but Zadeki's own erratic heartbeat and the sound of shallow breathing. There was a foul, rotting, rancid stench that threatened to take him hostage. But even those faded with time.

Pain seared through his shoulders and chest. Bands of cold metal rubbed against the skin of his ankles, wrists and neck, pinching and pulling power from his soul. His head throbbed, and his stomach wanted to empty. It was like the first days he'd been in the Greenstone South's crib room, only this was worse. Much, much worse.

Had he been abandoned to rot and die?

He held his breath and strained to listen to the ragged breathing beside him. He pushed out his mind-sense, surprised at how weak it was and shivered at the feeling of weight above him. Not like the caverns, not a mountain pressing down, but wherever he was, he was buried deeper than the grave.

There it was again, the sense of another life, somehow muted, contained, like a familiar scent.

'Who are you?' But the words stuck in his throat and came out as a rasp. He licked his cracked lips.

'Zadeki?' a pained whisper. 'Thank the Maker. I thought they'd killed you.'

'Baba?' Relief drenched him like cold water on a hot day. 'Are you alright?'

'Never better.' Baba croaked a laugh.

'And Aunt Bikan?'

A soft sigh told him his memories were true, that his da-baba's sister was dead. Zadeki had borne the edge of her sharp tongue on many occasions. He'd been terrified of her as a youngling, maybe still was. His breath caught. No, had been. Over the last several days, he'd seen another side to her as they'd flown together over the waves.

One minute alive, the next gone beyond recovering. Unbidden tears rolled down his cheeks. Maybe Aunt Bikan wouldn't have died if he'd followed her directions.

He strained against the dark metal, sending himself swaying and spinning, and thought of the forms he knew. While more powerful, the jaguar form wouldn't free him from the painful bite of the restraints without dislocating joints or making the bounds bite harder. Perhaps, in the eagle or the smaller macaw form, he could slip free and find a way to escape this black hole.

He willed the change to colourful bird and at once snapped back into his human form at the sudden deep disorientation. It was if his sense of self blurred and frayed like mist in a dark wind.

'Baba, can you get free?'

'Let me try.' A faint rustle and a sharp intake of breath. 'No, not safely. This dark metal acts against our abilities.'

'Then there is nothing we can do to escape.'

'We can keep hold of hope and wait for opportunity.'

The moments crawled by. Thirst and questions

tormented Zadeki. What had happened to Danel and Ariel? Had they escaped? Did Princess Avardin have Delvina as she claimed? Del wouldn't have betrayed them. She'd been different since the shipwreck, distracted, distant, almost cold at times, but she would not have done that. Besides it didn't make sense. She had tried to persuade Aunt Bikan to help the ebed. Or was Avardin the mysterious agent that fermented the rebellion? Had he and his kin been Avardin's price for cooperation?

'Where did you go when we were in the library, Baba?'

A long pause.

'Baba? Were you with the rebels?'

A dull clinking of chains moving. 'No. We spoke with the crystal singers.'

'For five days?'

'Yes,' Baba switched to the Filane tongue. 'Careful, son, the Vaane guards may be listening. We also spoke with the cantors of the Wayfarers."

'Why?'

Another long pause. 'The Kinleader has sensed a dark power deep in the caverns, tainting the mines. She had a hunch about its source and asked us to find answers while we were here.'

'And did you?'

'Da-Sestru also sensed the presence of shadow crystals in the mines, and perhaps even here, on the island.' A dull clank of moving chains. 'The crystal singers and the cantors confirmed these theories. And these dark chains prove it. They are a composite of rare iron and the shadow crystals, as ill-fated Iluien informed us. Glimmer crystals harness energy from the wind, the waves, the sun, and the deep rocks. Soul-bond crystals enhance the latent gifts of the Vaane. Shadow crystals restrain, subvert, bring under control. In the hands of the Sea Dragon King, or indeed, Princess Avardin who no doubt seeks her cousin's throne, such power would be disastrous.'

Zadeki mulled over Baba's words. 'Were you going to challenge the Council?'

'No. Elder Bikan decided we needed to return at once to tell the Kinleader what we had learned. We were coming to tell you when the watchers found us.'

'Aunt Bikan was so sure the mission would be successful, and now she is dead and we are soon to follow.'

'Zadeki, the plan is bigger than we are. We play our part to the best of our abilities.'

'But no one will learn what you found.'

'Bikan gave the Speaker an encoded message.'

Speaker? Oh Danel, but could the Darane escape the island without their help? And was it really his fate to die in this place, like this?

He felt the swing of the chains, the soft brush of Baba's arm against his. 'Youngest son, don't despair. You must be strong. Perhaps the dragon's daughter has abandoned us to die in this pit. Perhaps, she wants to question us.'

'I won't tell her anything.'

'Good. But remember, she has the Sea Dragon King's charisma gift. By the Maker's help you can resist it, if you don't allow the darkness to grow inside you.'

'I'll resist it, Baba.' Whatever happened, he wouldn't betray his people.

Tears tracked down Delvina's cheeks. She stood on the balcony, hardly seeing the flower gardens, fountains and the graceful shape of the aviary. Princess Avardin's extensive grounds had escaped the ravages of the rebel ebed, but beyond this peaceful haven thick smoke rose into the air over much of the city.

She gripped the balcony railings until it hurt. It had all been a farce, her childish dreams of a future with Zadeki, her excitement over her big adventure, and delusions about once again saving her realm. And though Avardin said she would help, the lady was preoccupied with discussions with the Council and subduing the rebels, bringing order to this privileged city.

'Would you like anything, Gentle?' Maia asked, her dark eyes questioning as she hovered in the doorway. 'Something to eat, perhaps?'

'No.' Eating was the last thing she felt like doing. She spun around. 'I want to go home.'

A harried look fluttered across the ebed's face. 'This is your home now.'

'No. Arghh! Just put the tray down and leave me alone.'

Maia dipped her head, 'Please eat, Lady Avardin insists you keep up your strength.'

The maid placed the tray on a small table and backed toward the open door.

Delvina frowned. Princess Avardin treated her with kindness and was more than generous but seemed overprotective. Would Maia help her find out what had happened to Zadeki ... and Danel and Ariel? She needed to know for sure.

'Wait.' Delvina strode across the room and grabbed Maia's arm, stopping her retreat. The young woman winced, her eyes flying open.

Delvina glanced down.

A purple-green bruise bloomed under the woman's ivory skin. Maia hurriedly pulled her flowing sleeves down, to cover up the injury.

'I ... I ran into a statue,' she breathed, eyes fastened on the floor.

'What happened to my friends?'

'I ... I do not know. I'm just an ebed. So many houses have burned.' She looked up, eyes imploring. 'Please, eat a little.'

'Why is it so important?" Delvina said without thinking.

'You are the Princess's new favourite. She ... she likes collecting exotic and unusual things.' Maia smoothed down her gauzy robe.

Delvina released a bitter laugh. 'I'm not exotic.' She thought of Ariel's elegant poise or the glacial beauty of the Princess. 'She is kind and wishes to help me, to help my people.'

Maia gave a tiny shake of her head, her soft brown hair swaying with the movement. 'No one else has such strange pale skin, no other ebed, and I've never seen such pretty grey eyes.' She clutched her trembling hands to her chest. 'You ... you shouldn't mistake the desire to acquire with kindness. She'll eventually tire of you, as she does with every other plaything. Not that there's much you can do ... just be wary.' And, as though she had said more than she meant to, she clasped her hand to her mouth and hurried away.

Delvina stared after her, feeling as if someone had punched her in the gut. Be wary. Those were Bikan's words. The Adelphi had betrayed her and Danel, used them. Or had they? Avardin said so. She also said that Danel and Ariel were dead. But she only had the

Princess's word for it, though Maia had said there were fires in the city. But ... but they could have survived.

She wasn't going to stand around waiting. She would find out for herself.

Delvina scooped up some rolls and fruit and added them to a pouch. She tiptoed through the maze of corridors, down the stairs to the lower floor. She crept past the downstairs reception room, where Avardin was discussing plans with Lord Hale and High Council members, and out a side door she had seen Maia and the other ebed use.

This time, she was glad the watchers at the gate barely looked at her. They shooed her on even before she finished saying she'd been sent on an errand. She gaped at the devastation in the streets; statues smashed, bushes trampled, windows shattered, houses burning. Watchers patrolled the streets, but one look at Avardin's insignia, and they waved her on.

She retraced the route to the Mariner's house and stood staring at the sodden mass of smoking ashes.

Her heart pounded painfully in her chest. How could it be true? Stalwart Danel with his love for the intricacies of buildings and fear of heights, gone just like that. It didn't bear thinking about. Even Ariel didn't deserve to die like this. Her chest felt hollow, her stomach leaden. And what had they done with Zadeki? She couldn't bear the idea of losing him so completely, his life cut short.

Surely someone there would have seen it if the Forest Folk had attacked the Council. Pulling her cloak across her face to filter the worst of the acrid smoke, she headed toward the city centre along the route she'd travelled back and forth for the last several days.

The closer she got to the Council Chambers, the less damage there was, and the more watchers. She was stopped a few times, but they waved her on. The temple and Council Chambers looked unchanged, though a crowd of silverskins and ebed thronged around the fountain in the plaza. Watchers waved off a flock of black birds with strong beaks swirling around something hanging on a pole in front the fountain.

A white cloth with dark red-brown stains fluttered in the wind. Silvery-white skin, dark hair unravelled. The body of a woman.

A shudder ran through Delvina and she gagged and heaved, leaving her weak and shaking at the sight of Highwun Bikan, cruelly slain.

Then, it was all true.

She turned and ran down the street, blinded by tears. People were looking at her. She slowed, ducked into the shadow of a building, gulped down great lungfuls of the smoky air. Pushing off the wall, she staggered on, one step after another, each one slower than the next.

She didn't want to go back to Avardin's pretty cage. She had to get back to the Glittering Realms, to tell Overseer Havilah and the others what had happened and what little they'd learnt about the seal. But how?

She frowned, vague memories of her conversation with Avardin in the aviary flitting just beyond reach. That whole afternoon was a hazy fog, but they'd talked about the seal. She remembered that. She had to think who could help her find a way home.

'Hey, you!' A watcher called out.

Scrubbing the tears from her eyes, Delvina turned back up the way she'd come, ran down a laneway and up a wide flight of stairs in front of her. A cloaked figure emerged from the shadows of the columns, grabbed her and pulled her inside.

Ariel woke to the jarring sound of marching boots in the laneway. She must have dozed off after being up most of the night fleeing the fire and tending to the ebed miner. The air in the shed was thick with smoke, dust and the smell of manure. She pushed the storage box firmer against the flimsy door and pulled the canvas cover over her and Danel. Pain shot through the burns on her hands.

A groan came from the miner.

'Hush.' She hissed.

Somewhere down the lane a child screamed, followed by shouting and a woman's loud wails.

The bootsteps moved closer, paused outside. Objects, probably truncheons, banged on the shed walls, shaking the structure. Someone opened the door, a blood-red light seeping through the cover.

Her heart squeezed tight and she held her breath, willing the Council's search squad to keep going. Moments dripped by.

'Nothing here. Move on.' And the stamp of boots on paved stone receded.

The ebed miner stirred. 'Thirsty. Hot.' He muttered.

Ariel picked up a water container and helped him drink. Half his face and his shoulder were swathed in bandages. It would take weeks for the burns to heal. But at least he seemed over the worst of the fever delirium. The herbal tonic was working.

His good eye snapped open. 'Where are we?' he croaked.

'Hush. Safe.' She murmured, though she doubted anyone was truly safe if the rumours were true. Rogue gangs of ebed still at large, the Grand Technician murdered, and Princess Avardin as good as regent. No word from Baba, though it would take more than a day or two with the roads barricaded and watchers rounding up anyone suspicious.

The shuffle of furtive steps outside. The door cracked open. Ariel gripped a stake, ready to defend herself.

'Gentle,' a familiar voice whispered and a dark figure crept in.

'Samwin!' Relief flooded through her. All the other ebed had fled, including Irina. 'Have you found out anything more?'

'Gentle, I don't know how much longer it will be safe to stay here. How is Danel? Is he still talking wild?'

'Hearing you.' The ebed miner struggled to sit up.

Ariel pushed him back on the blankets. 'You need rest.'

'Have you found the others? Delvina, Zadeki, the Forest Folk?'

'Maybe,' Samwin said. 'I think I saw Delvina walking toward the Council Chambers. She was in Princess Avardin's livery.'

'How is that possible?' Ariel mused. Would the Darane girl work with Avardin? What if the Princess had promised her something? 'Could she have betrayed us?'

'No, not Delvina,' her companion said. 'You don't know her like I do.'

'She spoke in defence of the rebels,' Ariel said.

Danel shook his head then grimaced with pain. 'She wouldn't betray us.'

'Gentle, you need to get to your father.' Samwin

twisted his hands together. 'The longer you wait, the greater the chance of discovery.'

Easier said than done. 'Tell me, Samwin, how are we going to get past the blockades and patrols? There's a bounty on our heads.'

'I can take you through the back streets, Gentle. They'll find you eventually if you stay here.'

'You go. Take the message with you.' Danel cradled his bandaged hands. 'I have to find Delvina first and the Forest Folk, if I can.'

'About that,' Samwin shifted his weight, rubbed his face. 'Gentle Bikan's body is in the square. There's naught you can do for them now.'

Ariel's hand flew to her mouth. Dead. The house burnt down. Patrols after them. Could the situation get any worse? Shivers ran up and down her spine.

Danel groaned, put his face in his hands. After a while he lifted his head, grim determination written across his face. 'I need to find Delvina. And if Bikan's body was the only one displayed, maybe Zadeki is alive.'

'It might be wise to check out how things stand before we head to Baba. Are you up to it?'

'Yes, Gentle Ariel. I'll walk across the ocean if I have to.'

Her father's ebed stirred. 'Gentle, I'm not sure that's—'

'Samwin, I've decided. You help ... er Danel.'

'Yes, Gentle,' Samwin put his arm under Danel's shoulders and helped him up.

They headed out into the haze. In the west, the sun was a burnished red disc through the thick haze, and night was already flowing into the smaller service streets between high buildings. In the east, the almost full moon was halfway up the darkened sky, her golden face a muddy red. They went slowly, in part to avoid running into patrols, but mostly because Danel was still very weak, leaning heavily on Samwin's shoulder.

They passed the back of the stables. 'Should we get the horses?' she whispered.

'The stables are guarded,' Samwin answered.

Ariel soon got lost in the maze of streets, starting with surprise when the octagonal bulk of the library with its circular dome loomed up in front of them. The towers and dome of the Council building loomed behind. Both looked different in the half-light and coming at them from this angle.

They followed Samwin down the lane to a small covered alcove.

Stay here while I scout around,' Samwin said. 'I asked my girl Nedrah to keep an eye on the Darane lass, if she could.'

Danel sank down on the cobbles and flopped against the wall. He ran a languid hand over the unbandaged part of his face. 'Thank you, Gentle Ariel.'

'What for?'

'For not turning me in.'

Ariel shook her head. 'Danel, you pulled me from the burning building. If it were not for you ...' She shook her head and shuddered. The doors had been barricaded. Only Danel and Samwin's quick thinking had saved them all. She would never forget Danel going back in again and again to bring out more ebed and in the end shielding the last one from the collapsing structure. She had been blinded all her life, dismissing the ebed as lesser beings. Danel and Samwin and the others had shamed her by their bravery. Maybe Zadeki had been right.

Tears trickled down her face and she swiped them away.

Danel's bandaged fingers brushed her wrist. 'It will turn out right, Gentle Ariel.'

'You can't know that.' She gave him a watery smile. 'But thank you.'

Two figures slipped in at the head of the lane and crept toward them. A patch of red-gold moonlight revealed their own house's livery and two familiar faces. 'Nedrah, do you know where Delvina is?'

'She was taken into the sanctuary, Gentle.'

'We can use the side entrance for ebed,' Samwin added.

He helped Danel up and led them further down the lane.

About halfway along, a small door on the side of the Wayfarer Shrine opened into a narrow corridor, past what looked like a robing room, and out into the long-pillared space of the sanctuary.

A short, stocky figure knelt before the altar, hair flaxen in the light of many flickering candles.

'Thank the powers, it's Del,' Danel almost shouted.

She turned, eyes wide, jumped up and ran towards them. 'Danel. You're alive.' She threw her arms around him.

'Ah, ah, careful,' Danel said.

'Are you hurt?'

'Just a few burns,' he grinned. 'I'll be alright.'

'They killed the Forest Folk.' She gave a little jump, as if noticing Ariel for the first time. 'Gentle,' she said.

Ariel gripped the hand of the young ebed woman in her uninjured one. 'We have to get you and Danel to safety.'

'May I help you?' A resonant voice came from behind them.

A robed and hooded cantor stood in front of a pillar. Ariel spun around, her legs turning to aspic. Please, let them not be discovered.

Samwin pulled a knife and Danel moved towards him, bandaged hands bunched into fists.

The cantor let his hood fall back and held up his hands. He was of medium height and thin, with light brown skin. 'Please, Gentles, I could not help overhearing.'

Samwin growled. 'Stay back! I don't want to hurt a servant of the temple.'

'Your secrets are safe with me, brother. I for one do not believe the lies that have been spread around. Sister Bikan and Brother Korak are peaceful followers of the Way.'

'Who are you?' Ariel demanded.

'Gentle Ariel, I am Aimlek, head cantor of this place.'

'I think he's okay,' Delvina said. 'He saved me from a watcher.'

'The Grand Technician sent an armed guard for the Forest Folk,' Danel rasped. 'Have you seen them?'

'They say all three were killed.'

Delvina let out a sob.

Ariel gripped the edge of the altar. Then it was true.

The Cantor continued. 'But only one body was displayed in the plaza and, when we asked, only one given to us for burial at sunset. A small army of watchers has been stationed outside abandoned cellars since midday yesterday.'

Delvina grabbed the Cantor's wrist. 'Is that where Zadeki and Korak are?'

'It's possible, child.'

Ariel shivered. 'We planned to leave the city tonight.' How could the five of them go up against the watchers?

Danel pulled himself straighter. 'We can't abandon them, if by any chance, they are alive.'

Ariel frowned. 'Gentle Bikan instructed us to find my father if they didn't return by nightfall. Don't you have to get information to your people?'

'That's little enough,' Delvina said. 'Danel can write a letter for Havilah for you to take. Whatever we do, we need to act before Avardin comes looking for me.'

The image of Zadeki's dark eyes, full of curiosity and laughter flashed before Ariel. Without the Forest Folk, they would never have made it through the gates in the storm or past the barricade, might never have made it to the island. 'Okay, let's try it then.'

Was she crazy? Most likely they'd be caught and tried for treachery. But the usurper Avardin had already labelled her as a traitor, burned down their house, and was hunting her through the city. If the shapeshifters lived, they could help. She had to do more than try.

Retza saluted the watchers stationed outside the ready room and marched through the door. Secondwun Timon was chalking up the next roster assignments on the duty board. Manoah sat in the corner, stacking ration packs.

Secondwun Timon glanced over his shoulder. 'Watcher Retza. Shouldn't you still be on shift?'

'I need to speak to Headwun Gilarth, sir.'

Manoah put down the pack he was working on and shuffled over.

'Don't say you got the high and mighty Lady Zara to talk,' he hooted.

Timon glared at him. 'That's enough, Watcher Manoah. I suggest you check to see if the prisoner's cells need cleaning.'

Manoah's joking face soured in an instant. 'Yes, sir.' He headed for the stairs to the holding cells.

Timon turned his gimlet stare to Retza. 'And this is important?'

'Yes, sir.'

'Headwun Gilarth's in a meeting in his ready room. So, is it related to Zara?'

'Yes, sir.'

'He'll want to know then. Go on in.'

Retza opened the door and entered the room, his muscles jangling. He hoped Gilarth would see his morsel of information as significant. Being demoted to cleaning duties or the third shift for a ten-day would suck.

Gilarth and Josenif were leaning over copper foils stretched on the table. Nebam sat on the corner of the table, arms folded across his narrow chest, one foot on the ground, the other swinging an agitated tempo.

'And you've searched the north and south mining outposts?' Josenif asked, his likeness to his younger brother, Zadeki, was striking.

Gilarth rubbed the back of his neck. 'A quick search of the main areas, the quartermaster stores and the farms. And that took long enough. There are thousands of lek of tunnels all up and we've had other matters to deal with. And our main aim at the time was to contain the Old Guard attacks. Which meant collapsing the tunnels connecting the different sections and also any of the older, worked-out sections in our area. I mean, where do you start?'

'You've got a ten-day before the Tamrin's pack yarmas arrive with food. Serafin might be able to fly some in or some people out … But maybe Zadeki's friend can tell us more?' Josenif turned and raised a flyaway eyebrow at Retza.

'Zadeki's friend?' Gilarth's thick eyebrows contracted. 'Oh?' He spun around. 'Watcher Retza, has she told you anything?'

Retza's legs turned to potato porridge and his mouth felt like a desert. 'Ah, yes, sir. I'm not sure how helpful it is.'

'Just spit it out, lad.'

'Lady Zara says the old Overseer might be at Temple's Rest.'

'Temple's Rest? Did she tell you where that is?'

'No, sir, she didn't know. The only temple I know of is the Sunken Temple.'

'Did you look there?' Nebam asked, his tone abrasive. The Secondwun's face looked haggard, his eyes hard and cynical. An abrasion on his temple disappeared into his pale ginger hairline.

Gilarth rubbed his square beard. 'Hmm, yes, sir. We searched it thoroughly and then closed it off by collapsing the access points as it has connections to the Overseer's quarters and the outer tunnels.'

'Are there temples in the other sectors?' Josenif asked. 'Perhaps this cryptic comment refers to one of those.'

Gilarth nodded. 'It's little enough to go on—'

'That's for sure,' Nebam muttered.

'—but it is worth checking out. I'll talk to Havilah

about it and Scrybe Barekia. The old scrybe knows more than anyone.'

Secondwun Nebam stood up. 'Make sure you report back to me.'

'Of course, sir.'

He turned and fixed Retza with an intense gaze. 'Are you sure she isn't holding back or misleading you, Prentice?'

Heat flooded Retza. It was several rosters since he'd been a prentice. Was Nebam trying to put him down? He swallowed down his ire. 'It's not like she was included in Uzza's councils.' He recalled the intensity of her eyes, the firmness of her tone. 'I think she's being honest.' But could he really be sure?

Secondwun Nebam gave a sharp nod and, without another word, walked out of the room.

Josenif gazed after him. 'Havilah's son seems troubled.'

Gilarth heaved a sigh. 'He's taken the failure of the tunnel attempt hard and blames himself for the collapse.'

'Is he at fault?'

Gilarth shrugged. 'He cut corners, but haven't we all taken calculated risks with time running out? I'll get together an expedition to follow-up this new lead. At least it's something.'

Josenif stepped back from the table and stretched. 'Good, in the meantime, show me where you know they have been. The trail will probably have gone cold even to jaguar senses after so many ten-days, but it's worth a try.'

'Yes, sure.' Gilarth turned to Retza and gave his shoulder a shake. 'Well done, lad. I knew you'd get the knowledge we needed.'

But it was so little. Nebam was right to be sceptical.

Still Retza could only hope it helped. At least they had a plan and with any luck, he would be chosen for the expedition.

'We need a plan.'

Delvina studied the other faces in dim shadows at the back of the Temple's main sanctuary. Danel's honest face half-hidden by bandages, with new lines etched in pain. Ariel's uncertain and mobile, as though she might change her mind at the first setback. Samwin's resigned and grimly determined. And Cantor Aimlek's seamed face displaying a mild curiosity and a practiced calm as he handed around small crusty loaves and clay bowls of a simple fish and seaweed stew. Could they trust this stranger? Not that they really had a choice now.

Outside, the muted sound of marching boots, the bark of commands and an occasional shout contrasted to the rustling quiet inside.

'We'll need more than a plan,' Samwin said. 'Nedrah says there are at least eight watchers guarding the entrance to the cellars, and archers stationed on the balconies above. There are countless more within call. It's going to take more than us few to overpower them.'

'By which time, you've roused the whole city,' Ariel muttered.

'Besides, the more people we bring into it, the greater the risk of betrayal.' Delvina picked at Avardin's livery, wishing she could pull it off and discard it like soiled rags. It was her fault the Forest Folk had been taken. Avardin had used her, used her confessions to collaborate Irina's testimony against her friends. 'Maybe ... could we pretend to be servants bringing food and water? Then, if we can release the Forest Folk, they could take out the guards and Korak could fly us to the cove.'

'It might work, provided they're not too injured,' Danel said.

Delvina's stomach clenched. What was Avardin doing to Zadeki and Korak? Would they be too late?

Samwin shrugged. 'You're the only one in the right livery. Though your accent might give you away. And they've allowed none but watchers in, as yet.'

Danel pushed his bowl away and stood up, swaying a little. 'I don't like it. Too risky.'

'You go on then, Thirdwun. I'm not leaving until Zadeki is ..,' her voice broke ...' is free.'

'Nor I,' Danel touched Delvina's shoulder. 'But we need a plan that works.'

The shouts and tramp of feet grew louder and a banging on the front doors rolled like thunder.

The Cantor jumped to his feet, his robe flapping. 'Quick, this way.' He hurried them through to another room. 'Help me with the chest.'

Given the urgency in the man's voice, Delvina grabbed the heavy chest without questions. With Samwin and Danel's help, they shifted it to one side.

Cantor Aimlek pulled up a trapdoor and thrust a small glimmer light into Delvina's hand. 'Hide in the secondary cellars. Sister Jossi and I will deal with the watchers.'

The stairs led down into the dark and at the bottom was a long corridor with doors on either side. Overhead came the scraping of the box being replaced.

They chose one of the rooms at random. Tiered shelves ran around three walls, stacked with cheeses, dusty sealed jugs, and other items.

'At least we won't starve down here,' Danel murmured.

With four of them, it was cramped, but it was probably too late to choose another room to hide in.

Above them, Delvina could hear the murmur of voices, shouted demands and the more peaceful replies of Cantor Aimlek. Delvina found an uncluttered spot and slipped down to sit on the rough stone floor. This was a little like home, surrounded by stone on six sides.

Even so, cave bats flittered inside Delvina's stomach. Would the Cantor betray them to Avardin? What did the Princess have planned for her, if she was recaptured? The memory of the bruise on Maia's slim arm set her heart racing. Was this beautiful and gracious woman really a monster, capable of deceit and betrayal to further her desire for power and possession? How could she have been so deceived as to believe Avardin was a friend?

Ariel stood, breathing rapidly, eyes as wide as two moons.

Samwin pulled out a crate. 'Sit, gentle. It's going to be alright.' He took a spot behind her, his hands fisting and unfisting.

Danel stood on the other side, running his bandaged hands over the brick wall. Though why, Delvina wasn't sure. There was nothing remarkable about the architecture of this stuffy room.

'Gentle, maybe we should turn off the light,' Samwin suggested.

The light would give them away, if the watchers did come this way, though by then, it would probably be too late. They had nowhere to escape to down here. Delvina pressed the switch. The soft blue light winked out, leaving them in a suffocating darkness.

Delvina held her breath waiting for the clanging above them to die down. As though that would help. The voices above muted before resuming after several heartbeats. Booted feet clumped, loud shouts and then a smashing sound. Finally, the voices and footsteps faded, as though leaving.

Silence, except for the ba-boom-ba-boom of her own heart.

Long moments slid by until a sliver of orange-yellow candlelight seeped under the door of the storeroom. Footsteps approached.

Delvina wished she had a hammer or even a messenger cylinder, but she could still kick and punch and bite. She wasn't going back to Avardin's gilded cage, if it killed her.

The door creaked open. Cantor Aimlek's long thin candlelit face stared at them. 'They've gone for now.' He shifted his owlish gaze to Delvina. 'They are looking for you, my dear. Princess Avardin has set a large reward for your capture.'

She took a breath and stood up. 'Right.' Whatever they did, they needed to do it soon. 'What if Ariel handed me in?'

'What?'

'To the watchers guarding the old cellars. And while they're distracted—'

'That's a crazy idea, Del,' Danel dropped his hands from the stone-brick wall.

'We've got to do something.'

'Yes, but we've been thinking like abovegrounders.' He beamed at her. 'I have another much better idea.'

A brilliant shaft of light blinded Zadeki, pulling him from half-dreams of feasting on fruit, fish and sava root cakes in the Great Forest. He squeezed his eyes shut and jerked against the metal collar holding his head. The movement sent him spinning on the chain, his arms pinned to his sides and his feet dangling.

A gust of hot smoky air filled the room, followed by the sound of boots descending.

He pushed open his eyes and blinked. A watcher stood at the bottom of the ladder. He pulled out a glimmer globe and hung it on a hook, then reached up to grab the overfilled water bucket that was being lowered to him.

The craving for moisture fired up inside Zadeki.

'Stinking shifters. Got to make you presentable for the new Regent.'

Cold water slammed into him, shocking the breath out of him and sending him swinging on the chain. Shudders ran through his body, igniting a fiery pain in his injured shoulder. He gasped for air and then remembered to lick his lips, sweeping up every drop of precious water on his desert-dry tongue.

'Now for the other one.' The watcher threw water over Baba, streams running over his head and body, splashing onto the stone below. '

That should do it,' the watcher above called down to his companion. 'Move aside for the Regent.'

More footsteps, lighter this time, and a shapely silhouette blocked the light. Avardin climbed down the stairs and stopped in front of him. She pulled a bouquet of small, fragrant flowers out of her sleeve and pressed it to her nose. Her opalescent eyes glittered in the artificial blue-white light.

'Lower the boy down.'

The watcher moved to a lever and depressed it.

The chain above Zadeki creaked and clanked and he dropped like a stone, only to be pulled up sharply, his bare feet mere ninas above the ground. He groaned at the jarring pain.

Avardin stepped forward, her long fingers stealing across his skin and seeming to find every bruise on his battered body.

'Quite impressive. You took some taking down, wild cub. How old are you? Less than fifty solars?'

Zadeki's flesh crawled. He focused on Baba's slow breathing and reassuring presence.

Avardin's hand gripped his chin, turning him on the chain to face her. Her eyes bored into his. 'They say it's possible to tame a wild cub if caught young enough, but I fear you are past that age.' Her eyes lingered. 'A pity.'

'What do you want with us?' Baba croaked.

The woman kept her eyes on Zadeki. 'Information, Korak. Can you tell me how many of you there are? How the ebed miners and the Tamrin are placed? Their strengths and weaknesses?' She raised her shapely eyebrows. 'I imagine you've increased in numbers over many decades since the pact with my late uncle, but as you see, I have found ways to counter your unnatural powers. A war between us would end quite differently. But, if you and yours cooperate with my plans, I'm sure we can come to some understanding. You will find me merciful, generous even.'

'You underestimate us, as did your uncle.'

'I thought this might be a challenge.' She ran a long fingernail along Zadeki's face, and a shiver ran through him.

She sighed and pulled a guava fruit from her robes. 'Would you like something to eat?'

Zadeki's mouth watered and almost without volition, he leaned toward the sweet smell.

'Tell me what I want to know, even a single fact, and I'll give you a bite.'

Zadeki pressed his lips together, wishing he could turn his head away from her mesmerising eyes.

'No?' She bit into the fruit. Pink juice ran down her chin. 'Not hungry enough yet? It's getting late and I have another tiresome meeting with the Council soon and a runaway ebed to deal with. I will be back to talk with you tomorrow. She dropped the half-eaten fruit on the ground and wiped her hand on Zadeki's chest.

'You.' She turned to face Baba. 'I'll leave you to think over my offer.'

'Don't waste your time. We will not be helping you extend your influence, daughter of shadows.'

Avardin's lips twisted into a predatory smile. 'Noble, but misguided.'

She held up a finger. The watchers struck Zadeki with a truncheon. His eyes watered as pain shot through him.

'I think our session tomorrow might be hard on your cub.'

'Take your savagery out on me,' Baba pleaded.

'And lose my leverage? Come, Korak. I may not be able to compel you, but perhaps for the love of your cub, you will submit to my rule. Do you think I enjoy this?'

Baba closed his eyes. 'I don't know what thoughts go on in your petrified heart.'

'Baba won't betray our Kin. No matter what you do to me.'

'For your sake, I hope you are wrong, little cub.'

Avardin turned to the guard. 'Get them a little broth. I don't want them dying in the night. Not yet.'

'Yes, Your Honour.'

The watcher followed Avardin up the ladder. The trapdoor banged shut, taking all the light with it.

Avardin's poisoned words churned around in Zadeki's mind. The only bright point was that he would take the brunt of the punishment. For now. How long before they died? Could he remain strong? He had survived being trapped under the mountain, but this was a thousand times worse. Where was the Maker in all this?

'Don't give up hope, son of my heart.' Zadeki wasn't sure whether Baba had spoken or the words where in his own head.

'I won't, Baba,' he whispered.

Zara divided a couple of dried mushrooms and a slither of algae cake into two bowls. Jesson's eyes, big and shadowed in his pale face, followed her movements as she poured hot water over the unappetising portions. Had she done the right thing in telling Retza about Temple's Rest? What would the rebels do to Baba and the other members of her family if they found them? But without food they would all die. That is, if Retza and Gilarth were telling the truth about the Gate.

She ducked her head and stirred. Her stomach cramped at the thought of yet more algae and she thought longingly of the fish from the previous day. She missed the variety of foods at her baba's table—grilled cave fish, crays, fat snails, potato cakes, and roasted birds with shaved tree roots.

She gave Jesson the bowl, and he slurped down the

green mess in one gulp. He wiped his mouth and lay down on the floor without his normal incessant chatter or restless energy. A couple of ten-days of half-rations had sapped their energy.

The metal spoon rattled against the rim of her bowl. She took a deep breath and slowly scooped the broth.

Outside, the sound of someone walking the corridors, then raised voices. Was one of them Retza's? The other had a sharper, more nasally tone. Not her business, probably. These days the watchers usually left her and Jesson alone for the whole shift.

A set of boot steps receded at a run. A moment of silence and the door flew open, slamming and rebounding against the wall.

A man in a toolwun's tunic and breeches instead of watcher-black stepped into the room. Pale ginger hair and scrappy beard framed his narrow face. Secondwun Nebam, the rebel Putarn's brother and Havilah's son. What was he doing here?

He shoved the door shut with his heel.

She stood up, her spoon clattering to the floor, and moved to shield Jesson.

'What do you want?'

He folded his arms and leant against the door. 'I want to open the Gate your da-baba sealed against us. I want the Overseer's seal, or a way to bypass it. I want you to tell us all you know.'

Her heartbeat ratcheted up at his cold, hard tone. 'I already told Watcher Retza what I know.'

'Really? Your baba is at Temple's Rest? And can you tell me where that is, by any chance? Did you make that up, all by yourself? Where is the seal!' Nebam took a step closer, his face flashing from a greyish tone to inflamed red. 'Tell me.'

'I ... I don't know where the Seal is or even what it is.'

'Wrong answer.' He took another step closer. 'Where would your father be hiding?'

'You leave my sister alone.' Jesson darted out from behind her, but Zara held him back. She didn't want him anywhere near Putarn's brother.

Nebam's eyes narrowed. 'We're just having a nice conversation, for now. I don't want to hurt you, but I will if I have to. All our lives depend on finding the seal and opening the Gate and you have the answers. So tell me, where is he, where is it?'

She shook her head until her teeth rattled. 'I don't know.' More boots pounded on the stone floor outside. Terror clawed at her throat. She wouldn't let them hurt Jesson.

'Try again.'

'Jesson and I are the youngest. It's not like we were told anything.'

The door smashed open. Gilarth barrelled through the doorway, Retza and Havilah on his heels.

Zara stepped backwards, pulling Jesson with her until she bumped into the table. Her breath came in quick spurts, her heart hammered like a battering ram. 'Don't hurt my brother, please.'

'No one is going to hurt you,' Havilah said, her face twisted with displeasure. 'Nebam, stand down.'

Nebam spun around. 'Don't you see? She's hiding vital information from us. We have to know.'

A look of great sorrow clouded Havilah's face. Tears shone in her eyes. 'Nebam, don't do this. I can't lose another son to this darkness. You are all I have left.'

His face crumpled. 'There will be no one left, Matu. Don't you understand.'

'Danel and Delvina will bring answers from the Lonely Isle in time, I'm sure of it.'

'If it's at all possible, she will,' Retza added, but was that a quaver of uncertainty in his voice. The situation must truly be desperate. 'Or we find this Temple's Rest.'

Zara gripped Jesson's hand, holding him close. 'Leave us alone. I've told you all I know.'

Jesson pushed away from her. 'I could try to open the Gate for them.'

'Jesson, no!'

Nebam snorted. 'I lost over ten good toolwuns trying and none of them got close and that's just the first gate. The traps and wards are impenetrable. We need the seal.'

'The Gate would open for me, like the Heart Crystals responded to Zara's touch.'

'Jesson, no, you don't know that. It's too dangerous.'

Her brother twisted around. 'But Zara, we have to at least try. I don't want everyone to die. Delvina and Retza helped us, remember.'

Zara stared at her brother, unable to speak. So brave. So naïve. Would it even be possible?

Gilarth knelt on one knee and put a hand on her brother's shoulder. 'Listen Jesson. Your sister is right. It is too dangerous and it's unlikely to work. But we value the offer.'

'Do we know it won't work? We know so little about the seal.' Nebam wrung his hands. Havilah gave her son a steely look. He closed his eyes and sighed. 'Not that I expect the boy to do it.'

'This is silly.' Zara clenched her hands, took a deep breath. What if it could work? 'I'll do it.'

'What, no!' Gilarth jumped up.

'It's a brave offer, Zara,' Havilah touched her hand.

'But, apart from the risk, you keep the Crystal Heart alive. We'll die quicker and in the dark if it fails.'

'You would still have Jesson. He is 'the Shepherd's seed' too. You must promise to look after him, if ... in case ...' She raised her chin. 'We have to try.'

Resolve solidified like ice inside her. Whatever they said, she would do this, if only to prove that she wasn't as spoiled and heartless as they seemed to think.

Stay strong. Stay true.

Zadeki sighed as the long moments hung like dust motes in the air. His muscles screamed with inaction, his head throbbed, his nose itched, but he couldn't move to scratch it. Images danced across his light-starved eyes. Aunt Bikan's eagle form falling from the balcony, her blood-stained body on the mosaic floor.

He shivered. No, not that.

Avardin's twisted smile, her compelling eyes willing him to trust her, the dark pressure of her mind, her promises to return.

Argh, no, not that.

Delvina's distressed face. What had Avardin meant, that Delvina had betrayed them? Del and Retza were his friends. Though he'd known them for such a short time, they were as close as sister and brother. It was a bond not easily broken. But something was troubling her. Why hadn't he asked her what it was? Too late now.

No, no, think of something else.

His matu bidding him farewell beneath the filtered green of the forest, the macaws taking flight from the seiba tree, river-otters playing in the silky waters of Bent river, Josenif and Benjim teasing him for some gaff or slip-up, the Kinleader's patient smile. He allowed himself to sink into the dreams of home until he could almost smell the rain-soaked air, the rich leaf litter and fragrant plants. He could hear the patter of raindrops on the canopy, the rustling of leaves in the wind, the scratching of small hidden creatures in the undergrowth.

Scrape, scrape, scrape.

A scratching noise came on the other side from the trapdoor. Was it rats? Or some other subterranean creature. He wished it would go away.

The trapdoor slammed open and he blinked against the rosy-red glow. Was it from the last rays of the dying sun or fires raging through the city? Or both. He couldn't tell, but either way it was probably night.

Two watchers came down the ladder, one carrying a bucket, the other carrying a glimmer globe. The second one placed the globe on the hook and pulled the trapdoor closed behind them. Zadeki braced himself for another dousing, though his hair remained damp from the last one.

The taller watcher pulled the lever and Zadeki dropped, not quite as far this time.

'Feeding time,' the shorter one said. He laughed.

'Let's just get this over with, Onaat.' The second watcher dipped a bowl in the bucket and lifted it to Zadeki's mouth.

A foul smell of rotted vegetables and rancid meat hit him like a blow. Despite the fact that his whole body craved food, he clamped his mouth shut.

'Now, now. The Princess says you have to eat.' Onaat clamped his fingers on Zadeki's nose and yanked his mouth open, while the other watcher tipped the foul smelling, lukewarm liquid in. Some of the liquid ran the wrong way and Zadeki coughed and spluttered.

Next, they lowered Baba and poured food down his throat, being none too gentle about it.

'Don't get too comfortable. Flame-get.' Onaat sneered. 'Gah, it stinks in here. '

Scrape. Scrape. Scrape.

'What is that?' Onaat said. 'Do you hear it, Jed?'

The other watcher scratched his head. 'Reckon there might be rats in here.'

'You mean in addition to these two sorry excuses for life?' Onaat sniggered. 'Better hope they don't get nibbled during the night.' He put his hand to the lever.

Zadeki's cheeks flamed. Had they no pity, no shame?

'Why do you follow Avardin against your oaths of loyalty to Prince Selwin and Grand Technician Iulien?' Baba asked, his voice quiet and measured.

Onaat backhanded Baba across the face. 'Shut your mouth, Flame-get. What would you know?'

The other one, Jed took the glimmer globe off the hook and angled it to shine into Baba's eyes. 'We are loyal to the heir, Prince Selwin. Princess Avardin has been appointed Regent after you killed the Grand Technician.'

'The Princess killed Iulien son of Gaian. Lord Hale and the rebel ebed helped her.'

'Liars. Don't listen to them, Jed.'

Scrape, scrape, scrape. The scratchings grew louder, closer and harder to ignore.

'And how long will your baby prince live with his cousin as Regent?' Was Baba trying to distract the watchers from the rat, or whatever it was tunnelling towards them?'

'I said, shut it,' growled Onaat.

Jed directed the globe to the wall behind Zadeki and Baba.

A soft thudding sound, like dirt falling, then a slide of stone on stone.

'Someone is trying to break in,' Jed breathed.

'Shush.' Onaat pulled out his truncheon and stepped closer.

Could it be? Zadeki's heart tripped and sped away like a frightened yarma.

'We should get the others down here.'

Jed grunted. 'I'll go. You stay here.'

'Nah, you stay here.'

Zadeki's chest squeezed. If his friends were trying to rescue them, they'd emerge into an ambush. He had to warn them. But how, when he was trussed up like a spider's meal.

Unless.

Zadeki moved his hips and chest muscles, swaying back and forth. Baba's eyes lit up and he followed Zadeki's lead.

The chain creaked and clanked. Onaat twisted around.

'What are you discards up to.'

Zadeki's chained legs rammed into him, pushing him into Jed. They both went down in a tangle of limbs, cursing and thrashing about. Jed pushed himself up first, but Baba rammed into him and he fell on top of Onaat with a curse.

Bang. Something heavy hit against the wall and bricks sprayed outwards, tumbling over the writhing watchers, pinning them down. The glimmer globe fell, smashing into fragments on the stone floor.

Everything went dark. More stone blocks fell and soft glimmerlight spread from a new cavity in the wall.

A dust-coated head poked out. 'They're in here.' A

gruff voice. Samwin. The ebed loosened some more stones and wriggled into the room.

Danel emerged behind him, face swathed in dust-coated bandages. And then Delvina, balancing a pickaxe in one hand and a glimmer torch in the other. Her eyes rounded as they met Zadeki's. She flushed. 'Are you alright?'

'Never better for seeing you three.'

In a rumbling series of crashes, a dazed Onaat clawed his way out from under the rubble, sending bricks scattering across the ground. Jed groaned and clutched his head, more bricks cascading down. He blinked his eyes like a light-confused owl.

'The guards,' Zadeki urged.

Delvina stepped forward and shone the torch in guards' eyes while Samwin charged Onaat, knocking the guard back down, this time landing on Jed. The air puffing out of both of them. That had to hurt.

Delvina waved the pickaxe over them. 'Keep still if you want to keep your skulls intact.' She looked at Baba then Danel. 'We should tie them up.'

'Let me,' Samwin tossed his knife to his left hand and pulled out rope attached to his belt. He proceeded to truss and gag the two watchers.

Danel leaned against the wall, his face strained. His head and hands were bandaged. But he was alive despite what Avardin had said, and here crwas Delvina saving the day. Zadeki grinned. Lies to confuse them.

Once the last knot was tied, Delvina handed Danel the pickaxe and looked around. 'How do we get you two down?'

'The levers over there, daughter of the mountain,' Baba twisted on his chain, pointing with his feet. 'Just be care—'

The chains squealed and Zadeki slammed into the ground.

'Ow!'

At least he'd only been a tanis or two off the floor.

'Sorry,' Delvina said. She took more care in lowering Baba. 'Now, how to get the chains off. We should have brought a chisel.'

'A stone might do the job,' Danel said.

'Or this.' Samwin pulled a key from Onaat's belt.

A banging came from above and the trapdoor opened a crack.

'What's taking so long down there? Do you need help?'

Samwin masked his voice with his hand and yelled back. 'Think a couple of no-hopers strung up like a highborn's dinner is going to cause us much strife? We're just having a bit of fun, mate.'

'Well, okay, but the Princess wants them alive remember.' The trapdoor slammed shut.

Samwin bent down and unlocked Zadeki's shackles.

Zadeki fell to his hands and feet. Fire screamed through every muscle and sinew. A long seeping groove ran along his shoulder, like an arrow graze, and his ear and the back of his head was painful and swollen.

'Aunt Bikan is dead.' He said, the reality of it hitting him like a cave-in again.

Delvina knelt next to him. 'We know. I'm so sorry. Come, we need to leave.'

Zadeki pushed himself up, grateful for Delvina's warm and steady presence.

'You take them back, Delvina' Danel said. 'We best backfill the hole.'

'No, you go with them Danel. You're injured.' Delvina said, 'Samwin and I will do it.'

Weariness weighed Danel down. He led the two surviving Forest Folk along the newly dug tunnel to the underground storerooms of the Temple. The expedition had taken more out of him than he was ready to concede, but they'd made it back. So far, so good.

Ariel and the two cantors hovered behind the piles of dirt and stone in the dimly-lit storeroom.

'Brother Korak,' Cantor Aimlek said. 'The Maker be praised.' He rushed forward and clasped Korak's hand before releasing it and then grabbed Zadeki's arm as the abovegrounder collapsed to the floor. The shapeshifters were bruised and battered, though Zadeki seemed particularly affected.

Danel didn't feel much better. The room swayed and pulsed, and his hands throbbed. He stumbled toward a box and sat down.

'You and your son need a healer and Danel too, by the looks of it,' Cantor Aimlek said. 'Sister Jossi here can fetch a healer.'

Korak shook his head. 'Too risky to delay. We need to get to Destruction Bay. Bring food and water and any herbs, ointments or bandages you have.'

'Are you sure? You won't get far in your current condition.'

Korak helped Zadeki to sit, placing a hand on his son's shoulder and closing his eyes. 'Please, if you could bring what I asked for.'

'As you wish, Gentle' He turned to the other cantor. 'Sister Jossi, stay with them.'

Ariel piped up. 'How are we going to get past the

watchers? They'll have even more patrols once they realise the flam ... er, the Forest Folk are missing.'

The Gentle's voice seemed to boom and fade. Scintillating, pulsing pinpricks of light flowed at the edges of Danel's vision. Every breath hurt, every word rasped his throat. The cantor was right. He wasn't up to travel, but someone had to get the message back.

'I've had it,' he mumbled. 'Can you make sure Delvina gets back to Havilah, however much she protests?' He slumped forward, head between his knees. 'I could distract the search.'

A firm, gentle hand gripped his shoulder. 'We're not leaving you behind, son of grit. Here, let me see your hands.' Korak helped him sit back against the wall and unwrapped the blood-stained bandages. His touch was cool, gentle, calming. 'Ariel, bring the water.'

'Shouldn't you be resting.'

'Our bodies heal faster than yours, though it would help if we could eat. These are nasty burns.' Korak opened his mouth and sang a lilting song of sunshine, green leaves and flowing water.

Danel's skin tingled and itched under the shapeshifters touch.

'That will do until Brother Aimlek comes back.' Korak slid down the wall to sit next to Zadeki.

Delvina still wasn't here. The jagged hole in the wall remained empty. Surely, she didn't plan to fill in the whole tunnel. They didn't have time. Danel pushed down the thought that she and Samwin had been discovered. They couldn't stay here much longer. They had to risk moving. But it seemed an impossible task to get back to the bay without running into the watchers now on high alert and patrolling the city.

Soon after, the Cantor and a companion bustled into the room, arms full of food, bandages and medical supplies. Aimlek placed food and water in front of the shapeshifters and moved over to Danel to tend his burns with soothing balms and clean bandages.

'Eat, my brother, friend.' Another cantor with light-brown skin pushed a honeyed roll into his newly bandaged hands.

'Are you ebed?'

Cantor Jossi smiled. She handed him a beaker of water. 'Vaane, ebed, high-born, low-born, such distinctions are not important in the Way. Now eat.'

Danel bit into the crusty bread and savoured the rich smoky honey smeared on it. He felt stronger and his mind clearer, from the moment the shapeshifter had touched him.

Korak and Zadeki were eating with a steady focus, while Ariel nibbled at a roll, her eyes darting around the room.

A rumbling from the tunnel and Samwin and Delvina emerged, coated in earth and rock dust.

'You took your time,' Danel said.

Delvina rubbed at the dark shadows under her eyes. 'We've bricked up the wall and backfilled a bit. Should brick up this side too.'

'Don't worry about it. My brothers and sisters can do it, and we'll rearrange the shelving. It will be morning soon.'

'We should be going.' Korak said, his voice stronger. He popped another roll into his mouth. It was amazing how much food the Forest Folk could eat when they put their minds to it. Already, he looked less gaunt, and the purpling under his silver skin seemed less intense.

Danel leaned forward. 'You need a plan.'

'We, you mean.' Zadeki waved a hand, a bit of his old bravado showing through. 'We're not leaving without you, even if we have to carry you.'

'Yes, but how can we get out of Silantis without being caught?'

'It's a pity we can't dig all the way to the cove.' Delvina sighed. 'It would take days.'

'If we could dig to the city limits ...' Danel pulled his beard. But even that would be punishing, and they would be trapped if the watchers discovered the entrance. If only he had Greenstone South crew with him and some firepower.

Korak swallowed a last bite and brushed the crumbs from his hands. 'Is the tunnel to the burial place of the old kings and queens intact?'

'The Sea Dragon King blocked those off many years ...' Cantor Aimlek's voice faded. Excitement lit in his dark grey eyes. 'The tunnel started at the Temple and led to the ravine below the slopes of Mount Kilwah, which is just ten lek north to Destruction Bay.' The man's wrinkled face sobered. 'It would be a fitting place to lay Gentle Bikan to rest, unless you can suggest a better place?'

Sorrow and grief washed over Korak's face and Zadeki turned toward the wall.

'Avardin gave you her body to tend?'

'She refused but we stole it from the plaza. It is shameful to treat a daughter of the Flame King in such a way.'

'Or any one of the Maker's children.' Korak ran a hand over his face. 'Better the mountain ravine than buried in cellars.' Tears ran down Korak's cheeks. 'Can we see her. Jazadek and I will sing over her.'

'I respect your loss, but ... do you have time?' Ariel asked.

'We will be brief, but this we should do. Danel, can you or Delvina see if the way can be opened? Go when you are ready, go on without us and we can catch up.'

Danel pushed himself up. 'Of course, Highwun.' Though if he could help it, he wasn't leaving the Forest Folk behind again.

The tunnel opened out into a narrow valley, a sharp rift in the side of the large conical hill. The sun had slid above the dense forest at the end of the long ravine. Close by, a waterfall fell into a swirling pond, before running out into a stream. Bird calls rang through the stillness. To Delvina it felt like a place long forgotten. She paused as the others stepped out into the dewy half-light of dawn.

Zadeki and Korak still hadn't come.

She understood their need to mourn Highwun Bikan, but she hoped they'd hurry, that they didn't get caught in Avardin's net again.

'Don't worry, Runner Delvina. We're not leaving until they catch us up.' Danel moved toward her. He looked stronger and in less pain.

She smiled back, warmth spreading across her cheeks.

'Where are these tombs?' Ariel's clear voice sent nearby birds scattering into the air.

They walked down a green, mossy path following the flow of the stream. A glittering cobalt-blue insect with transparent wings hovered over the smooth flow. A few paces away, a white stone foot jutted out from a mass of foliage. Delvina pushed the fan-like leaves aside to reveal a statue of a tall slender woman.

'I think this is the burial place,' she said.

Statues of tall men and women draped in vegetation, perhaps seven in all lined both sides of the ravine.

'Queen Sheva,' said a quiet voice behind her. She whirled around, her heart jumping through her chest.

Korak and Zadeki stood, eyes clear and the bruises beneath their skin developing a greenish-brown tinge, as though sustained days ago.

'Are these your people?' Danel asked. 'Didn't Aimlek mention you are descended from Kings?'

'The Flame King. Though, he was more Kinleader than tyrant.'

'This is why the Sea Dragon King hated you?'

'One of the reasons. He desired to rule for the wrong reasons. And he cared not how he obtained that rule.'

Ariel spun round, eyes wide. 'Do you mean to depose Avardin and the young prince to take the rule back?'

Highwun Korak held up both hands. 'No, no, no. Even if your people would accept us, which I doubt. This is no longer our calling. You Vaane—highborn, gentles and ebed alike—must seek a way to live together in fairness and harmony. But come, we need to get to the cove before Avardin remembers there is a ship waiting.'

Samwin rubbed the back of his neck. 'It's at least half a day's walk.'

'If you can climb to the ridge up there, I'll get you to the White Rose before midday,' Korak said.

'Can you carry four of us, and so soon after your ordeal?' Delvina wondered.

Samwin cleared his throat. 'Three.'

Everyone looked at him.

'With your permission, Gentle Ariel, I'll return to the city.'

'No, it's too dangerous!'

'Brother Korak is right. It is up to us to deal with Avardin. She would not have as much support if it were known she, and not the … the Forest Folk … killed the Grand Technician.'

Ariel brightened. 'Then I shall go with you. We will do this together.'

'No, Gentle, you should go to your father and tell him all that has happened.'

Ariel sighed then touched Samwin's hand. 'Please forgive me my arrogance.'

Samwin ducked his head and nodded. 'Of course.'

'And after I've spoken to Baba, I'll join you. Korak is also right. We need to work together to defeat Avardin.'

A small smile lit Samwin's face and his eyes brightened. He took Ariel's hand in two of his own. 'It would be an honour to fight beside you.' He turned back and walked back down the ravine.

Korak called out after them. 'May the Maker go with you, friend Samwin.'

Danel cleared his throat. 'How do we get to the top?'

'Come, there should be some stairs.' Highwun Korak walked along the stream, then bounded over it. 'Ah there. Come, let's get going.'

The narrow stairs cut deep into the side of the mountain, climbing steeply. Delvina was winded by the time they reached the top. While dense bushes and trees hugged the sides of the mountain, the area below the summit was grass and bare rock. Below them, the island stretched out like a Tamrin tapestry edged in a sparkling line of blue. In the east, trails of smoke sat over the enclosed bay and the sprawling city of Silantis. The south remained clear. For now.

Korak walked toward a flattish area near the summit. He leapt into the air, his form stretching and changing into his koraktil-form, perhaps a bit scrawnier than the last time but still magnificent. He landed on four sturdy legs like a jaguar and opened wide wings, halfway between bat and bird.

Ariel clapped a hand to her mouth. 'A flame breather. Why didn't you use that form against Avardin?'

The koraktil shook its great head. 'Space ...' He hesitated a moment. '... and my injuries and the dark metal worked against such a difficult form. Enough talk. Mount up.'

Delvina jumped up on the hind leg and scrambled onto Korak's broad back. Danel followed, despite his bandaged hands. No harness this time.

Ariel stood still, feet firmly on the ground and her robe and hair tugged by the wind.

'Don't worry, I can rope you on.' Zadeki took her hand with a grin and half-carried half-shoved her onto the space behind Danel.

A niggle squirmed in Delvina's chest, but then she squashed it. How could she resent Ariel, when it was her own actions that had almost brought them all to ruin and led to Highwun Bikan's death?

Zadeki tightened the last knot. 'There, that should do it.'

'Aren't you coming too?' Ariel asked in a breathless tone.

He rubbed and stretched his shoulder and grinned. 'I should be able to fly on my own.'

His gaze caught Delvina's. With a flourish, closer to his old cheerful self, he ran down the slope and leapt off a precipice head first.

Ariel squawked.

Even as he fell, Zadeki's shape shimmered and changed into a crested eagle with outspread wings.

At the same time, Korak's muscles bunched beneath them. 'Hang on.'

Danel's hands gripped tighter and he breathed in sharply. 'Here we go.'

The Highwun ran along the ridge and jumped off after his son.

Ariel squealed louder.

Delvina's stomach dropped as they plummeted down toward the ravine. One, two, three. The great beat of outstretched wings thrummed the air currents. With a few powerful heart-stopping strokes, they climbed toward the wispy clouds. Mount Kilwah's crater and wooded ravines spread out before them.

Stronger in the heights, the wind buffeted against them and threatened to pull them adrift. Delvina was glad that, without harness and saddle, Zadeki had thought to bring the rope.

Soon the wooded slopes gave way to fields of spelt and hummocky grass, farm houses and small villages. Then the dark grey crescent of sand and the muted roar of waves and the sting of salty air signalled their arrival at the bay.

The White Rose bobbed on dark blue water fringed with white waves, both masts straight and true. Delvina's spirits lifted. Had it been that easy?

As Korak swooped lower, she could make out people on the beach. Watchers and ship's crew fighting. Her heart wilted. They were too late. Avardin had caught up with them.

'Hold on tight,' Korak roared. He tilted at a steep angle, speeding toward the fighting like an arrow. His chest swelled beneath them, and with a whoosh, flames spurted out of his mouth and nostrils, setting the grass on fire behind Avardin's forces. The watchers yelled, and men scattered. Horses bolted. Habbiah's crew charged after them.

'Son of the waves, get to the boat,' Korak roared at Habbiah.

Korak looped back, swooped lower and picked up a watcher with a leader's insignia in his front claws. The man kicked and screamed. Several lengths away, Korak dropped him in the waves before circling back.

Zadeki swooped and dove at the watchers' faces, distracting them and allowing Habbiah's crew to overcome their opponents.

'Retreat, retreat.' The black-clad watchers stumbled and fled through the tussocky grasses.

'To the ship,' Mariner Habbiah called. The sailors threw off the few remaining attackers and jumped into the boats, rowing toward the White Rose.

Korak wheeled around once more, sending flames after the retreating watchers. 'For Bikan daughter of Telsima,' he roared.

Delvina shivered at the fierceness in his voice. Once roused, the Adelphi would be a terrible foe. She was relieved they were usually a peaceful folk.

'Can we get to the boat now?' Delvina managed to say. Her fingers cramped from hanging on. Danel held her tight, his breath hot on the back of her neck. 'Ariel, are you alright?' she called back.

'Yes,' came the weak reply. 'I … I think I'm about to slip off.'

'Grab hold of me,' Danel called out.

Korak turned, slower now, and landed on the deck of the ship, almost taking the whole space.

Delvina waited until Ariel and Danel had dismounted before sliding off the soft furred body. Zadeki landed behind them, changing seamlessly into his human form.

'Why didn't you do that in Silantis?' Ariel huffed, 'Instead of walking through the tunnels.'

'No height, besides the towers have koraktil-killing arrows,' Korak huffed as he transformed back to human size and shape. 'Ah, now I'm hungry again. Better take a bite before the Mariner gets here and we need to guide the ship through the Grinder.' He headed toward the galley.

Danel and Ariel followed him, but Delvina lingered. A hand fell on her shoulder.

'Hey, Del.' Zadeki said, 'You've been avoiding me.'

Delvina jumped, feeling a spike of guilt. 'No, why do you say that?' She turned and met Zadeki's intense gaze.

'Have I done something wrong?' He asked, then sighed when she did not answer. 'Oh, well, perhaps one day you'll be ready to tell me.' He turned away, shoulders slumped, a weary stumble in his steps.

She blinked the tears blurring her sight. She ran and caught his arm. He turned, an eyebrow raised.

'I told Avardin everything. It's my fault you were captured and ....' She couldn't say it.

His dark eyebrows dipped down. 'She said you'd betrayed us. But why? I don't understand.'

Delvina swallowed the lump in her throat. 'I didn't mean to. I trusted her and ... and I was angry with you and Ariel. But it's not your fault.' There, she'd said it.

He tilted his head, forehead scrunched. 'Ariel?' His eyes sprung wider. 'You don't mean ...'

Delvina hung her head. 'It's okay. If you two, you know, want to ... I'm happy for you.'

'So that's what Avardin meant.' Zadeki shook his head. 'Del, I'm sorry I've been so dense, but I'm not ready to have a family or be tied down just yet. I want to be a pathfinder, explore the wide land. Besides, I ...' A shadow flitted across his face, like a cloud passing over the terrain. He took a deep breath. 'But if I was looking for a mate, I'd choose you over a hundred Ariels. You are kind, generous, brave and strong ...'

Delvina's cheeks burned. She looked at the silly slippers Avardin had made her wear.

'... and beautiful.'

'Don't tease me.' She pushed his shoulder.

'Ouch. That hurt. I'm not. I mean it.'

'How can you say that after ... what I did?'

'You made a mistake. So did I. Telsima's daughter would still be alive, but for me. At least now I understand why you've been so distant.' He gave a sad smile. 'I guess being friends isn't enough.'

The ship deck shuddered as a small boat nudged against the side. Crew ran to help pull the craft up. Overhead, seabirds swirled and cawed amongst the rigging. Delvina stood welded to the deck, not knowing what to say.

'Looks like the Mariner is back on board. Better eat before my next transformation. I'm still a bit weak. Be safe, Runner Delvina.' He turned to walk down the deck.

Were her wounded feelings worth losing his friendship?

She ran after him. 'Zadeki.'

'What?'

'No reason we can't still be friends, right? Like a brother and sister.'

'Sure.' He grinned back at her, his dark eyes sparkling

like a star-filled sky. Yet there was still a shadow that hadn't been there before. Whatever words she said couldn't bring Highwun Bikan back. Couldn't change what happened in the Hole. Couldn't change the fact she'd almost betrayed everything and everybody she loved.

But he'd not held her mistakes against her. A new day with all its possibilities lay before them.

'I always wanted a younger sister.' He pulled her into a tight hug, kissing the top her head and then let her go.

'I thought I was older than you.' She sighed. 'We came all this way, for nothing.'

'No, we have learnt something about transferring the authority of seals and ... and soul-bound crystals. Avardin would have done what she did without your help. It may have taken her longer, but perhaps we've given Samwin and Ariel hope too. I think it might make a difference.'

Was that enough? By the Maker's favour, it would have to be. For now, she would focus on returning to the Glittering Realms with the knowledge they had acquired at such cost.

Things would never be the same again, but a small ember of hope still glowed bright in the dark.

Zara walked towards the ebony gate, the first of seven. The hair prickled on the back of her neck. She didn't need to turn to know that the eyes of Havilah, Gilarth and Retza watched each careful step she made. She took a steadying breath and willed one foot to step in front on the other. Long strands of cobwebs waved in the downdraft of a nearby ventilation shaft. The dim light of glimmer torches shimmered on layers of thick dust and grunge disturbed only by boot prints leading towards the door but not away from it. What made her think this was a good idea? Just because the glimmer crystals were now attuned to her, didn't mean whatever wards and traps her father had placed on the Gate would not harm her. But she had to try, if only to prove herself to these prickly toolwuns that she did care about the fate of the realm. But mostly, for Jesson ... and Retza. She rubbed her moist hands down her skirt and continued walking.

TO BE CONTINED

Author Note

Caverns of the Deep, the final book in the Under the Mountain series, is now available.

For news on new releases – sign up to the Jeanette O'Hagan Writes monthly newsletter http://eepurl.com/bbLJKT

Or check out my website JeanetteOHagan.com), Facebook author page (Jeanette O'Hagan Author and Speaker), on Twitter (@JeanetteOHagan), Instagram (bythelightof2moons), or Goodreads (Jeanette O'Hagan). I'm also on Pinterest, Bookbub and Linkedin.

Enjoyed this story from the world of Nardva? Please leave a fair and honest review on Amazon, Goodreads and/or your favourite reviewing site.

You might also like:
Caverns of the Deep – the fifth and final book in the Under the Mountain series
Akrad's Children–book one in the Akrad's Legacy series
Ruhanna's Flight and other stories — a collection of short stories, mostly set in Nardva

Coming Soon
Rasel's Song–the book 2 in the Akrad's Legacy series –2019/2020
Chameleon Protocols trilogy 2020/2021.

Acknowledgements

Shadow Crystals is the fourth novella in the Under the Mountain series, with the next novella Caverns of the Deep, completing the series. When I first started to write a short story based on the theme 'glimpses of light', I had no idea how far it would carry me. From delving deep into the dark corners of a mining realm, to the edges of the Great Forest of the Forest Folk, and even across the ocean to the Lonely Isles. These places were already a reality from plotting and daydreaming the *Akrad's Legacy* series (of which only *Akrad's Children* has so far been published), but it has been exhilarating to explore them in greater detail and in a different time period. And Delvina, Retza and Zadeki have wormed their way into my heart.

Writing isn't a solitary pastime. I am especially grateful to my critique-partners, beta-readers, editors and proof readers who have helped me polish and refine my work. So many people and places have been an inspiration for my world building, from the mines of Mt Isa to a couple of voyages across the Indian Ocean, to rainforests of my homeland, among books and movies and research.

Special thanks to my sister Kathleen Hillenberg who is such an enthusiastic and untiring supporter and has given great feedback on practically every story I've written. Also Suzanne Hay-Bartlem, Nola Passmore, Lynne Stringer, Raelene Purtill, Adam Collings, Cate McKeown, Linsey Painter and Neasa Nic Dhómhnaill.

Nola Passmore of *The Write Flourish* is a fantastic editor and I love her work.

I'm grateful for my family—my loving husband Tony, my precious children Kathleen and David, my parents Tom and Jean Curtis—who instilled in me a love of faith and fantasy—and siblings, Tom Curtis, Frank Curtis, Chris Curtis and Kathleen Hillenberg, with whom I've shared many wonderful adventures.

Most of all, I'm grateful to my Maker in whose creative footsteps I can only hope to follow.

Jeanette O'Hagan 6 February 2019

About the Author

Jeanette O'Hagan enjoys writing fiction, poetry, blogging and editing. She is writing her *Akrad's Legacy Series*—a Young Adult secondary world fantasy fiction with adventure, courtly intrigue and romantic elements. Her short stories and poems are published in a number of anthologies including *The Quantum Soul, Tales From the Underground, Futurevision* and *Glimpses of Light*. She has published now four novellas in the *Under the Mountain* series, her debut novel *Akrad's Children* and a collection of short stories, *Ruhanna's Flight and other stories*.

Jeanette has practised medicine, studied communication, history, theology and, more recently, a Master's in writing. She is a member of a number of writers' groups. She loves reading, painting, travel, catching up for coffee with friends and pondering the meaning of life. Jeanette lives in Brisbane with her husband and children.

Publications

Novels

Akrad's Legacy series
Akrad's Children (By the Light Books, 2017)
Rasel's Song – due 2019/2020
Mannok's Betrayal – due 2020

Novellas

Under the Mountain series:
Heart of the Mountain: a short novella (By the Light Books, 2016)
Blood Crystal: a novella (By the Light Books, 2017)
Stone of the Sea: a novella – (By the Light Books, 2018)
Shadow Crystals: a novella – (By the Light Books, 2019)
Caverns of the Deep: a novella — due May/June 2019

Short Stories

Tamrin Tales/Tales of the South:
Ruhanna's Flight and other stories, (By the Light Books, 2018)
'Shadows of the Deep' in Tales From the Underground, (Inklings Press, 2017)
'The Herbalist's Daughter' (By the Light Books, 2016; originally in Tied in Pink romance anthology, (Far Horizons, 2014)
'Lakwi's Lament' (By the Light Books, 2017) originally in Like a Girl Plan anthology, (Far Horizons, 2015)
'Withered Seeds' in Redemption (WAG, 2017)
'Treasure in the Snow' in From the Edge (WAG, 2019)

Barrakan Tales/Tales of the North:
'Broken Promises' in Another Time Another Place anthology, (Swinburne Students, 2015);

'Full Moon Rises' in Like a Woman anthology, edited by Mirren Hogan, Jeanette O'Hagan and Christina Aitken (Mirren Hogan, 2017)

'Stasia's Stand' in Crossroads, edited Lynn Fowler (Birdcatcher Books, 2017)

'Wolf Scout' in Tales of Magic and Destiny (Inklings Press, 2019)

Science-Fiction:
'Space Junk' in Mixed Blessings: Genre-lly Speaking, (Breath of Fresh Air Press: 2016)

'Rendezvous at Alexgaia' in Futurevision, edited Delia Strange (1231 Publishing, 2017)

'Project Chameleon' in The Quantum Soul, (Sci-Fi Roundtable, 2017)

'Rookie Mistake' and 'Eating Time' in Mixed Blessings: As Time Goes By, edited by Deb Porter (Breath of Press Air Press, 2017)

'Maroon's Sanctuary' in Gods of Clay (Sci-Fi Roundtable, 2019)

'Space Triage' in Challenge Accepted (Stephanie Barr, 2019)

Links and updates can be found at her website
Jeanette O'Hagan Writes http://jeanetteohagan.com
or her email newsletter http://eepurl.com/bbLJKT

Caverns of the Deep

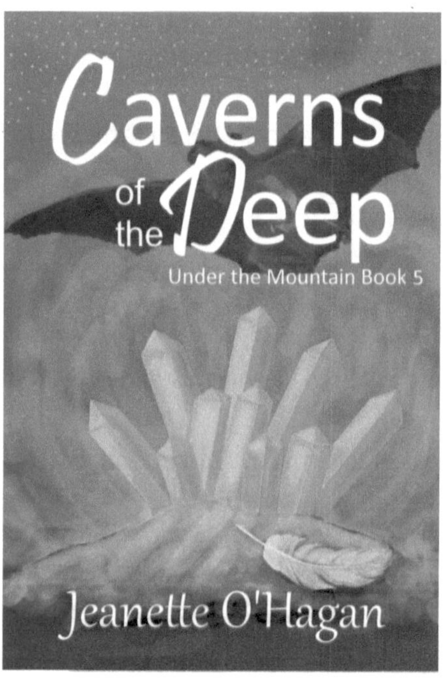

Seven Gates, locked and warded, stand between life and starvation. Danger and betrayal stalk the tunnels and shadows grow darker in the deep caverns beneath the mountain. Will Zadeki, Zara, Danel and the twins (Retza and Delvina) find a way to save the Glittering Realms and secure a better future?

Caverns of the Deep is the exciting finale to *Heart of the Mountain*.

Available on Amazon and other retailers:
https://books2read.com/u/mgGeBv

Akrad's Children

Caught between two cultures, a pawn in a deadly power struggle, Dinnis longs for the day his father will rescue him and his sister from the sorcerer Akrad's clutches. But things don't turn out how Dinnis imagines and his father betrays him. Will he seek revenge for wrongs like his sister or forge a different destiny?

Akrad's Children is the first book in the Akrad's Legacy series

Available on Amazon and other retailers:
http://books2read.com/u/31xWMM

Ruhanna's Flight and other Stories

Ruhanna's Flight and other stories includes previously pubished and brand new stories set in the world of Nardva. A delightful introduction to Jeanette O'Hagan's fantasy world of engaging characters and stirring adventures.

"This author has the gift of immersing a reader in a different world and caring about the people in the world." Amazon Review.

Available on Amazon and other retailers:
http://books2read.com/u/mKKeJE